Truelove's Journal

TRUELOVE'S JOURNAL

A Bookshop Novella

Ralph St John Featherstonehaugh

 BooksUlster

First published in digital format 2012

Paperback edition published in 2014 by Books Ulster.
Text reset, with minor alterations, in 2017.

The author © 2017

ISBN: 978-1-910375-05-1

Cover illustration by Maria Becvar

Contents

Acknowledgments

I would like to thank the following who have in one way or another contributed towards the publication of this book: Anne Smyth, David Aimer, Penny Kennedy, Peter Tafuri and Lindsey Malcolm.

For Lovers and Booklovers

When You are Old

When you are old and gray and full of sleep,
And nodding by the fire, take down this book,
And slowly read, and dream of the soft look
Your eyes had once, and of their shadows deep;

How many loved your moments of glad grace,
And loved your beauty with love false or true;
But one man loved the pilgrim soul in you,
And loved the sorrows of your changing face;

And bending down beside the glowing bars,
Murmur, a little sadly, how love fled
And paced upon the mountains overhead
And hid his face amid a crowd of stars.

William Butler Yeats

Chapter I

A Discovery

I had long expected the day to be a memorable one in my life, but it was to prove more profoundly momentous than I had anticipated.

With a modest bequest from my mother, added to what I had put by over the course of more than ten years in employment, I had invested in a small commercial property on the periphery of the town centre.

Working in a dead-end office job had been tolerable enough for some years, but eventually I began to grow weary of the dull routine and lack of challenge. The tedium increased steadily, until it got to the stage where I could scarcely raise myself from bed in the morning, knowing only too well what the day would bring. I was determined to escape while still a young man, but to what I had no idea.

Countless times I had passed that estate agent window on the High Street and never so much as paused to glance in its direction. Then, on my way home one Wednesday afternoon, I stopped almost involuntarily before it and found my eyes drawn to the photograph of a quaint little

double-fronted shop. 'Prime commercial premises —
Close to town centre — Ground floor shop with living
accommodation above — In need of modernisation', the
advertisement read. In some inexplicable, irrational way,
I felt that I had just kept an appointment with fate.

Three months later the shop was legally mine.

Standing proudly before it with the keys in my hand, I
looked up at the previous owner's wooden sign, which was
painted in gold lettering on a black background:

'G. J. Truelove, Bookseller — Est. 1969 — Books
bought & sold'.

The paint was cracked and peeling and the sign in need
of general repair, but that was of no consequence now. I
would replace it with a modern weatherproof one that
would require no more than an occasional wipe, and would
be more in keeping with the trendy image I had in mind.

Everything I had was to be staked on this venture, so I
needed to get it up and running as quickly as possible. I
had to start earning before debt started to accrue, but, up
to the eleventh hour before completion of the sale, I still
hadn't decided on what to sell. The difficulty was that I
had no experience with, knowledge of, or even passion for
anything in particular.

Knowing that I wanted to work for myself and deciding
to buy the shop had been the easy bit. Thinking of what I
should sell was another matter altogether. Nothing obvious

had sprung to mind, and I agonized over the question for some time before eventually resigning myself to men's fashion wear. At least I knew something about clothes, I reasoned — I wore them, after all. Besides, I was aware that young men liked to spend a high proportion of their disposable income on looking the part, so how far wrong could I go? Mistakes would undoubtedly be made, but hopefully they would be early and inconsequential and I would learn the trade quickly enough to survive.

I stepped into the tapered recess between the two windows and unlocked the shop door for the very first time. A little bell tinkled agreeably as I entered, and I paused immediately inside to survey what was before me, and to savour for a moment that sweet feeling of new ownership.

Viewed through the eyes of anyone other than an excited novice the scene might have proved rather deflating. The walls could not have seen a coat of paint in decades, and they were pockmarked with holes in the plaster where securing nails for the shelving had been ripped carelessly from their beds. The abandoned carpet had been poorly cut and fitted and, for the most part, failed to reach the edges. It was stained, strewn with animal hair, and dotted with cigarette burns and blackened blobs of trampled-in chewing gum; and regular routes had been worn to a sheen by innumerable book-browsing footfalls. The debris of a hasty clearance lay scattered across its surface: a torn dustjacket, a bookmark, a shattered biro, and miscellaneous coins. Stripped of all but its shabby carpet, the old shop seemed so jaded and sad. There was a fusty smell of neglect about it too, somewhat mitigated by the aroma of fresh coffee wafting in from the café next door.

To my right was a connecting door that opened into the hallway of the upstairs accommodation. It was a plain plywood affair that had the word 'Private' crudely hand-painted on it in white. Beside it was an old Bakelite light switch that I went over to and flipped aimlessly, knowing perfectly well that the power was disconnected.

I pottered about for a while, thinking how I might best fit and furnish the shop for my chosen business. I considered things like what type of fittings I might use on the walls, how many clothes rails could realistically be squeezed into the floor space, and where the till ought to be positioned. I would like to have replaced the deep double windows with a more fashionable flat frontage, but that would come at considerable expense and, after paying for the essential renovations and modernisation, it wasn't likely that I'd even come near to being able to afford it.

At the back of the shop, in the right-hand corner, was the entrance to the store. The door had been removed from its jamb and replaced by a multi-coloured strip blind that rustled pleasantly as I passed through and stepped down to the cold concrete floor. Immediately on the left was the door to the yard and, on the same side, set in a mildewed wall, was a begrimed window comprised of a fixed pane flanked by casements, both of which were now seized shut. The wall opposite the window had, as in the shop, been crudely stripped of shelving, rendering the room entirely bare and desolate.

I leaned into the dank and dingy little room at the far end of the store. In it was housed an old-fashioned pull-chain toilet, with its ceramic cistern mounted high on the back wall. A pool of murky water lay stagnant in the grimy little wash-hand basin, unable to drain any faster than it was being replenished by a slow, regular, plopping drip from the cold water tap. In the near corner stood a garden spade with the price label still on its varnished shaft, and, beside it, a tired looking broom with bent and unevenly worn bristles, its head secured to the handle by means of a crooked nail.

I went outside to complete the downstairs tour. The yard was L-shaped, being long and narrow the length of the store and toilet, with its tail formed by a rectangular grassy patch behind the end of the building. Lying rather incongruously in the middle of this miniature wilderness of grass and weed was a small, elongated boulder.

On feeling the first spits of incipient rain I was prompted to return indoors. I was impatient to see upstairs anyhow and, since it would be my home for the foreseeable future, I was particularly keen to look around it at my leisure, a luxury which being unaccompanied for the first time would afford me.

As I parted the strip curtain and stepped back into the shop, I happened to glimpse a shelved recess inside a little alcove to my left, and on those shelves were stacked a number of large hardback notebooks. Through idle curiosity I pulled one out at random and discovered it to be a volume of the bookseller's diary.

The emotional journey that would change my life began with the leafing of pages in Truelove's journal.

Chapter II

A New Dawn

AWN was breaking by the time I finished reading, and I felt drained and bereft, as though I had just lost a very dear friend.

I cannot recall what first caught my attention in the journal, but I started to read the occasional entry with more than a passing interest, until I gradually got drawn deeper and deeper in. If I'd stopped to think about it at the time this would have greatly surprised me, as I was by no means a bookish person, and, to my eternal shame, I probably hadn't opened a book in earnest since English Literature classes at school.

It was evident from Truelove's writing that books were more than just a means to earn his keep, more than even a pleasure to him, but his whole world, his *raison d'être*. He made comments and critiques on books that he had read, noting why they were worthy, and what he had learned from them; he remarked on the quality of illustrations, the aesthetics of bindings, the quirkiness of customers, and on every aspect of books and bookshop life. This was a man who had an all-consuming passion for his trade, and I envied him that.

At some point I decided to go back to the beginning to see how it had all started for him. The volumes had been hand-numbered on their spines, so I pulled out the first one and turned to the initial page. The journal opened with an account of the shop's inaugural day, which, in Truelove's own words, had got off to a 'painfully slow and quiet start'. Not a sinner passed through the door in over two hours. Faces would occasionally appear at the window, then suddenly flit away and be gone. A solitary soul eventually made his way in, browsed indifferently for a while, then left without a word. Meanwhile Truelove tried to read, but was too tense to focus properly. He would not be able to relax until that first sale had been made. As time went on his tension increased. A few more people drifted in and back out again, but still no sale came. It was almost as if the would-be customers sensed his desperation and it frightened them off. But, come lunchtime, the shop began to fill, and as though some kind of communal feeling of safety in numbers came to prevail, the browsers seemed much more at their ease.

Then, finally, the breakthrough came. A young lady lifted a book from the window and made her way purposefully towards him. She handed over a copy of *The Chess Players* by Frances Parkinson Keyes, and this, therefore, was the first title that Truelove was destined to sell. It was a book that he himself had read, without intending to; but the blurb on the jacket flap led him to the first chapter, and the first chapter led to the second, the second to the third, and from there he read on without interruption until the final page was turned. Based on the life of Paul Morphy, the American chess master, the story had held the bookseller enthralled. His mind boggled at the genius of the man who, in 1858, had played eight very capable chess players simultaneously in the Café de La Régence in Paris, winning six of the games and drawing two; and, as if that wasn't enough, Morphy did it blindfolded, with his back to his opponents. At the end he appeared as fresh as when he started, as though it had scarcely been a challenge at all.

The floodgates seemed to open after that and one transaction quickly followed another. Truelove had stocked the shop partly from lots that he'd bought from recent house auctions, but mostly with books that he'd read and amassed over the years, so that many of those that sold were old favourites to him. Among them was Ernle Bradford's *The Great Siege: Malta 1565*, another book that he had found impossible to put down. He read agog of how the Knights of the Order of St John of Jerusalem had defended the island from the besieging Ottoman army of Suleiman the Magnificent, noting wryly that it was not a book for those of a delicate disposition; because this was far from a gentleman's conflict, but a bloody no-quarter-given battle in which the decapitated heads of prisoners were fired back into the enemy's camp by cannon.

By way of contrast, *The Trachtenberg Speed System of Basic Mathematics*, sold to a bespectacled and rather studious looking young man, demonstrates how much more useful a head can be when still attached to its body. For Trachtenberg was able to develop his astounding method of making rapid and complex arithmetical calculations while he was incarcerated in a Nazi concentration camp. He constructed the system entirely in his mind, under the harshest of conditions, and without the aid of books, paper, pen or pencil. Reading the book was a humbling experience for the bookseller. Given a forest of paper, and a hundred years, he knew that he himself could not have come close to achieving the same.

But the crowning glory of the day, in many respects, was the sale of *The Complete Newgate Calendar*, published in five volumes by the Navarre Society in 1926. Truelove had passed many an entertaining hour pouring over the stories of the various rogues and rapscallions who had been imprisoned in Newgate and executed at Tyburn. All human vice and every form of crime was to be found within those pages — housebreaking, highway robbery, bigamy, blackmail, forgery, arson, grave-robbing, pickpocketing, piracy, murder, of course, and even cannibalism. But there was bathos, pathos and humour in them too, and the bookseller, despite himself, could not help but appreciate the audacity and ingenuity of many of the perpetrators. How could he fail to admire the boy who trained a sparrow to aid him in his burglaries; or the man who taught his dog to pick pockets; or not marvel at the highwayman who escaped prison by faking death by the plague and then reappeared on the roads as his own ghost; or not be amused by the quack who feigned treason in order to gain a free ride to London at His Majesty's expense? The law officers laughed so hard at his impudence that they decided to let him go with a caution. In the bottom right-hand corner of the dustwrappers was a quotation from *The Beggar's Opera* in which the character Peachum states 'The World, my Dear, hath not such a Contempt for Roguery as you imagine.' How very true; and, as far as Truelove was concerned, the gentleman who had paid for the set in ten shilling notes could not have invested his money more rewardingly.

All in all, despite the shaky start, it ultimately proved to be a thoroughly satisfactory day of trading, and it continued well in the following days too.

That first week just flew by for Truelove.

On the Friday, an elderly lady came in and asked for a copy of *Poems by Christina Rossetti*, but in a specific edition, illustrated by Florence Harrison. She had been given the book as a present when a young girl, and had read it eagerly, delighting in the beautiful colour plates; however, when her family fled to England to escape the Irish Civil War of the early 1920s, she had sadly been parted from it. For almost fifty years she had enquired after a replacement in every second-hand bookshop that she came across, though all to no avail. Then, on spotting Truelove's shop from the window of a bus a couple of days previously, she determined to visit it at the first opportunity. The book she sought was by no means common, but by one of those strange quirks of fate, or perhaps merely through the laws of probability, the bookseller just happened to have acquired a copy as part of a lot from a recent auction. Her eyes lit up when he handed it to her; but, a moment later, she became tearful and emotional, causing the bookseller to feel not a little awkward and embarrassed.

'I'm sorry, dear,' she said, on gathering herself, 'But it's just that I've had a bit of a shock.'

When she had turned to the front of the book — there — on the flyleaf — in her father's own copperplate handwriting — was the gift inscription that he had so lovingly written to her more than half a century before.

In progressing through the volumes of the bookseller's journal it became increasingly apparent that there was a particular poignancy connected with the world of second-hand books. As with the old lady who had been long parted from a cherished volume of poetry, people frequently formed bonds with books because of their association with other people, places and times, and the loss of these books could in some degree be likened to a minor bereavement. Truelove often experienced a bitter sweetness in buying the collections of departed booklovers. From their books he came to understand who they were, almost as though he'd known them personally, and it was a constant reminder to him of the ephemeral nature of life and his own mortality. At times he pondered on what the point of reading might be if, at the point of death, all one's accumulated knowledge just ceases to exist. For a long time he periodically struggled to come to terms with the idea that all that learning might be entirely futile, until eventually he was struck by what he felt should have been obvious to him all along — that, if nothing else, reading deeply enriches a life in a way that only the true bibliophile can fully appreciate, and that is reward and justification in itself.

Almost sadder than obtaining books by death was their acquisition through blindness. Too often the bookseller had been called to houses to clear the collections of those who could no longer see to lift a familiar book from its shelf and revisit the joys that they had once found within its pages. He could only begin to imagine how soul destroying that might be, and fervently hoped that his heart would cease beating long before his own eyesight should fail.

Truelove's Journal

The purchasing of old family bibles, in which were often recorded births, deaths and marriages, was another source of disquiet to Truelove, because the implication was either that the family line had come to an end or, worse still, that the inheriting descendant valued his forbears and ancestry at no more than a handful of pounds. Beautiful as some of these bibles were, in their finely tooled leather bindings and with their handsome brass clasps, the resale price was far from commensurate with the craftsmanship or genealogical value of the books.

I had read for some hours seated on the floor but, as darkness began to envelop me, I lifted the volumes of the journal and clambered into a dais at the front of the shop in order to gain the last vestiges of light coming through the whitewashed window. When this too became inadequate, I was determined to find a means to continue reading, for by that stage I had reached the beginning of an intriguing story, and one that I was impatient to see through to its conclusion.

Chapter III

Ghosts

I entered the hallway to the flat through the connecting door and climbed the short flight of stairs that led to a small rectangular half-landing, off the far side of which was the rather antiquated bathroom.

A further step up in the opposite direction brought me to the main landing, where wooden balustrades continued to flank me on the left before twisting again at the far end into another flight of stairs that ran directly above and parallel to the first, ascending to an attic bedroom and box-room. To my right, as I reached the end of the landing, was the entrance to the compact little kitchen and, straight ahead, the doorway to the sitting room, my intended destination.

Dusk was by this stage rapidly thickening into darkness and the world about me was now just shades and shapes, cloaking the story that the room had to tell. I had read that story before on previous visits, only perfunctorily and without attachment. This time, revisiting the detail from memory, those traces of the bookseller's life were imbued with a meaning and an emotional significance that had hitherto been absent for me.

In daylight I had seen how the once white wallpaper and ceiling had yellowed considerably with age, a process hastened and deepened no doubt by the absorption of innumerable plumes of tobacco smoke. On the party wall, to the left of the door as one entered, was a brighter patch, that together with a rectangular impression left on the carpet at its foot, betrayed the fact that some sort of tall unit had until recently stood against it. From the context of the story it was not difficult to imagine what this might have been, but, like everything else of any monetary value in the building, the bookcase had been removed for sale, leaving only the entirely worthless fittings for the new owner — me — to dispose of.

The electrical fixtures were from another age. The light switch, blackened around the periphery by countless mis-placed fingertip impressions, was a bulbous contraption, shaped somewhat like a chocolate tea-cake, with a chunky little on-off lever in the centre. Emerging from the ceiling rose was an intertwined dual flex, covered by a woven fabric of a serviceable brown hue, that terminated in a shade-less and bulbless Bakelite fitting. There was only one socket for the whole room, and that was designed for appliances with round pin plugs that had long since had their day. There was neither television aerial nor phone point. The electrics, on a different circuit to the shop, had packed in many years previously, and rather than face the intrusion and expense of having them repaired, the bookseller had chosen to forego their use in this his retreat from the world.

Against the wall behind the door sat an abandoned and rather forlorn green settee, the arms plucked into a perfect fluffiness. The three sorry-looking cushions were supported by a sheet of plywood in lieu of springs that had apparently succumbed to critical fatigue. Housed in the opposite wall were two sash windows that overlooked the street, both veiled by lifelessly grey net curtains that had been tacked into place at the top.

Beneath my feet was an old-fashioned patterned carpet, strewn with animal hair, and worn to its hessian backing in the centre. Towards the hearth it was pock-marked where hot coals explosively ejected from the fire had landed, and in the grate remained the cinders and ashes of a final fire. As I approached the fireplace the headlamps of a passing car illuminated the upper half of the wall, momentarily throwing the objects on the mantelpiece into sharp relief. In the brief instant before the vehicle quickly swished past on the rain-sodden road below, I saw at one end a round glass ashtray, overflowing with hand-rolled cigarette butts, and, at the other, what I had come for and what I presumed would still be there — a wax-flooded saucer and two spare candles.

All the while I was in the room I had a strange sense that I was not alone, that there was an awareness of my presence, as though I was being watched, but I shrugged this off as being purely the product of an overheightened imagination. I then cautiously made my way into the kitchen and felt about in the wall-mounted cupboard until my hand alighted on the box of matches that I remembered seeing there.

With matches, saucer and candles, I made my way downstairs again and back into the window dais of the shop. The bookseller had been in the habit of replacing dead matches into the matchbox, so I had to feel around for those with live heads, but the first couple I found simply crumbled between my fingertips. Damp had insinuated its way into the box, so I unsuccessfully struck one match after another until there was nothing left of the heads to strike. I began to despair of getting a light when, between the last half-head and a corner of the striking pad, enough friction was gained to produce a fizzing, spluttering flare. I quickly dipped the match downwards so that the flame would better catch the wood and, when I was sure it had taken, I levelled it again and applied it to the wick of one of the candles. Melting the wax in the saucer, I placed the candle in its middle, and read on through the journal by candlelight until the very last page had been turned.

Chapter IV

Bookselling

I N the 1830s a Spanish monk called Don Vincente became so obsessed with books that he took advantage of
the political upheaval of the day to plunder several monas-
tic libraries, including his own, of some their more valuable
volumes and manuscripts. He subsequently vanished for
a while before eventually reappearing as the proprietor of
a bookshop in Barcelona.

Then, on the death of its owner, a copy of *Furs e ordina-
cions* came up for auction. Printed in 1482 by Lamberto
Palmart, the first Spanish printer, it was believed to be the
only copy in existence, and Don Vincente was determined
to have it. He put up everything he owned in an effort to
secure it, but was nevertheless outbid by a rival collector.
In such circumstances he did what any self-respecting bib-
liomaniac would do — he stole the book and burned his
rival's house to the ground, with his rival in it.

The book was later discovered in a search of Don
Vincente's premises, but he might yet have got away with the
felony. Another copy had turned up in Paris, and his lawyer
argued that as there were two copies in existence then there

could conceivably be three or even more. There was no way of proving that the one in Don Vincente's possession had been stolen from his rival's house. However, Don Vincente was so distraught to learn that his was not the only copy that he took no further pains to conceal his guilt. He confessed to his crime and was executed at Barcelona in 1836.

Truelove was never as dangerously obsessed by books as Don Vincente, but neither did he become as disenchanted with them as George Orwell had. In 1936 Orwell published an essay called *Bookshop Memories* in which he wrote of his experiences as an assistant in a London bookshop. His disillusionment with bookselling largely derived from the seemingly endless stream of nuisances who came through the door, and not least from those who insisted on having books held over, never to return. Truelove avoided that irritation simply by refusing to do it, except for regular customers, or in special circumstances.

There was, for example, a middle-aged lady who spent her days wandering the streets of the town, wheeling a shopping trolley behind her. Her long frizzy hair was bunched together at the back with a clip, and she invariably wore a brilliant shade of red lipstick. She always dressed in the same green anorak and sported a long, multi-coloured scarf around her neck, and had her trousers tucked into a pair of green Wellington boots. As she tramped along, randomly touching objects as she went, her eyes would

be permanently fixed on the ground, scanning for money
that had fallen from purses and pockets. On days when it
looked unlikely to rain, Truelove would put an old trestle
table on the pavement in front of shop on which he would
place boxes of cheap books for passers-by to rummage
through and, from time to time, she would buy something
from these. She never spoke, but would simply show him
what she had taken, hand over the exact change, put the
book in her trolley, and disappear into the street again.
But then, on a first and only occasion, she came into the
shop, lifted a book from the window, and mumbled a
request to hold it aside for her. The books from the boxes
were nothings, worth mere pennies, and so Truelove had
not worried unduly about taking her money; however, the
one from the window was several pounds, and he balked
at the idea of charging her for it. So he waved her away as
a means of saying 'take it, no charge', but she nevertheless
stood her ground and continued to hold the book out to
him. When he realised that he was offending against her
dignity he took the book from her and asked:

'What name shall I put on it?'

She replied so softly, almost in a whisper, that he could
barely make out what she said, but he was fairly sure that
he heard 'Christmas Eve' and so that was what he wrote
on the bag into which he placed the book.

Christmas Eve returned within a couple of days and paid

for the book with a handful of assorted silver and copper.

Another source of annoyance to Orwell were the pretentious fools who were more interested in a book for its prestige or monetary value than its contents, or 'first edition snobs' as he called them. Truelove was of a like mind to Orwell on this. He had become a collector himself, but more by accident rather than by design. Whenever he came across books about books he would read them eagerly and then find himself reluctant to see them go, regardless of their apparent worth or lack of worth. He felt, like Arthur Conan Doyle in *Through the Magic Door*, that each had become like an old friend:

> Come through the magic door with me, and sit here on the green settee, where you can see the old oak case with its untidy lines of volumes. Smoking is not forbidden. Would you care to hear me talk of them? Well, I ask nothing better, for there is no volume there which is not a dear, personal friend, and what can a man talk of more pleasantly than that?

Where Truelove disagreed with Orwell was in the author's assertion that booksellers have to tell lies. Perhaps Orwell had been put in that position because he was an employee, but Truelove was his own master and refused to engage in any sort of sales patter, or even to recommend books. He left it entirely to the customer to find what he wanted and, if he didn't, then it was of little concern to him. Even when specifically asked for a title that he knew he had in stock he didn't necessarily make an effort to produce it. People often asked for books that they didn't actually want. Why, he had no idea, but he used his experience to first assess the genuineness of the enquiry before attempting to help. Truelove empathised with Orwell in his contempt for the variety of pests who seem particularly drawn to bookshops, but it hadn't destroyed his love for books or the bookselling business in the same way. He didn't suffer fools gladly, and over time he developed techniques to deal with them. He eventually came to operate on the principle that the customer was always wrong until he or she could prove otherwise, and that is probably what kept him sane and saved him from despondency.

It is hardly surprising that the bookseller gained a reputation for being a taciturn man of a thoroughly serious disposition, but that belied the fact that he had a most keen sense of humour. His journal was replete with witty and wry comments, and his true character was reflected in the books he enjoyed and remarked upon most.

Perhaps his favourite book on books was *The Private Papers of a Bankrupt Bookseller,* a humorous but fictional journal in which the bookshop owner reflects on literature, love and life. The Bankrupt Bookseller started out with such enthusiasm, optimism, and the loftiest of idealism for his chosen profession:

I am a bookseller. I am not a bookseller born and bred. I am one who has come late to the craft, but, if late, not less lovingly. Books are a transcript of life, they say, but to me they are more than the transcript. They are Life itself, for as it was in the Beginning — is now — and ever shall be, 'in the beginning was the Word'.

Towards the end it was a different story altogether. Under the heading 'The White Flag' he writes:

Some days this bookselling is the very torture of the devil. To-day has been such a day. I have done nothing right. I burnt myself with my aluminium kettle this morning. Two unpleasant and impatient demands for money were all that my morning post contained. A querulous old man has cancelled an order for a useless book without rhyme or reason and I am landed with what will be indubitably more bad stock. A miss — a minx, I might have written — tormented me about some novel she had heard of at a tennis party but she could neither tell me publisher, author, title, or give me an indication as to contents. 'You ought to know if you are a bookseller. Everybody's reading it just now.' *Hell!* The world defeats me and my head is both bloody and bowed. My fighting spirit is dead. I wonder what it is really like in the workhouse. Is it so bad after all?

The Bankrupt Bookseller's head began in the clouds and ended up in a gas oven at the back of his shop.

Books Fatal to Their Authors was another source of great amusement for Truelove. He laughed out loud when he read of the deluded author Quirinus Kuhlmann, who was prone to visions and mad ravings, and was ignominiously chased from one country to another:

> He then proceeded to Turkey on his mission, and presented himself to the Sultan. Although ignorant of the language of the country, he persuaded himself that he could speak in any tongue; but when they led him into the presence of the Sultan he waited in vain for the burning words of eloquence to flow. The Turks dealt with him according to his folly, and bestowed on him a sound thrashing.

With slips of paper Truelove had religiously book-marked every reference to bookselling and collecting in Robert Chambers' *Book of Days*, but the quotation that had pleased him most in the two volume set was a bookseller's bequest from 1785:

> I, Charles Parker, of New Bond Street, Middlesex, book-seller, give to Elizabeth Parker, the sum of £50, whom, through my foolish fondness, I made my wife, without regard to family, fame, or fortune; and who, in return, has not spared, most unjustly, to accuse me of every crime regarding human nature, save highway-robbery.

Despite the image the outside world may have had of him, Truelove most certainly had his lighter side. I knew from the outset that he was dead, because that was the reason given for the property coming on to the market. It was cruelly frustrating to think that I might have passed him on the street and not known who he was. I also felt a deep sense of regret at never having had occasion to seek out the bookshop when he was still alive. Through his journal I got to know the man in a way surpassed by only one other person, and that story began where the silk bookmark had been placed.

Chapter V

Socrates

IT wasn't until his second week in the shop that Truelove discovered that the refuse collection was on a Tuesday morning. Tilting the cylindrical metal bin slightly towards him, he used the base lip as a makeshift wheel to roll it along the yard and through the gate, which he had opened in preparation. As he placed it against the exterior of the yard wall, he noticed a rather emaciated black and white kitten trotting towards him, head bobbing as it came. When he returned to the yard and turned to close the gate behind him, the kitten was sitting facing him, its mouth open in a silent, supplicating miaow.

Truelove neither liked nor disliked cats. He had no experience of them on which to form an opinion one way or the other. They were, in fact, really a matter of complete indifference to him. However, although I think it is safe to say that he was not a particularly sentimental man, the bookseller would see neither man nor beast go hungry, and it wasn't difficult to deduce that this small beast was in want of food.

'Wait there!' he said.

Leaving the doors open behind him, he made his way back through the shop and climbed the flight of stairs to the flat. As he turned on the half-landing he saw the kitten sitting at the bottom of the stairs, looking quizzically up at him. By the time he got to the kitchen door it had reached the main landing and was following him along with its tail raised in the air like an aerial.

Truelove opened the kitchen cupboard and took out a tin of tuna that he had earmarked for his teatime sandwiches. As he applied an opener to the can, the kitten moved backwards and forwards, brushing sleekly against his leg in anticipation. Shovelling half the contents onto a saucer with a fork, he placed the food on the floor and watched as the kitten devoured it voraciously. Not until the whole tin had been polished off did the animal seem sated, and at that point it quickly rolled over and sprang agilely to its feet again, eliciting an inner smile from the bookseller. Thinking that the creature might also be thirsty he lifted a bottle from the refrigerator (which was a bucket of cold water kept under the sink) and presented the kitten with a saucer of milk. This, too, was readily received and quickly disposed of.

Having fed and watered the animal, he wasn't quite sure what to do next. He didn't want to force it out, so decided that the best policy would be to leave the doors open and let it go of its own accord. He set about his business as usual but, wherever he went, the kitten was never too far behind, and appeared to be in no big hurry to escape. Come opening time it was still hanging around, investigating nooks and crannies, plucking at the carpet, and sometimes bolting off at lightning speed to nowhere in particular and for no apparent reason. When the first customers entered it made itself scarce, retreating to the store for further investigation or to engage in a little cleaning and preening. As the day progressed it discovered the pleasure of sunbathing in the window and for some hours stretched lazily over the books on display, much to the amusement of passers-by.

In the late afternoon Truelove saw it saunter past his desk and disappear through the newly fitted strip blinds and into the store. At closing time there was no sign of it anywhere, so, believing that it was finally gone, he locked up at the front and had just done likewise with the yard door, when all of a sudden it reappeared on the outside ledge of the store window. Momentarily he was tempted to ignore it and just walk away, but found that he was unable to coldly abandon the animal, knowing that it could be hungry again and that he might well be its only source of sustenance. He opened a casement window and allowed it to jump down onto the stack of books heaped precariously against the lower wall.

That evening, having fed his visitor again with cat food

hastily purchased from the corner shop, Truelove settled down to do some reading. As he lay on the settee with a book propped up on his chest, the kitten decided to clamber on board and interpose itself between book and reader. It began to gently butt the bookseller's face and knead at his cardigan, purring contentedly as it did so. Rather disconcerted by this feline intimacy, and not quite knowing what to do, Truelove raised the book up and attempted to read on regardless, until the kitten eventually settled itself under his chin and across his neck.

When it came time to retire for the night he left the cat lying on the settee and made his way upstairs and into bed as usual. He had just reached a state of pleasant drowsiness when he felt his face being nudged, followed by a needle-like plying on his neck. No matter how many times he pushed it away, his affectionate assailant kept coming back to resume where it had left off, so Truelove ultimately resigned himself to waiting out this nesting process. It ended with the kitten lying so close to his face that he was half suffocated, but too afraid to move in case the nuzzling and kneading might begin again. Awkward as his position was, Truelove nonetheless experienced a novel sort of comfort in it.

For several days the bookseller fully expected his guest to move on at any time, but when it was still in residence after more than a week, he said:

'Well, if you're going to be staying, I suppose we ought to think of a name for you.'

But, try as he might, he failed to come up with anything appropriate. Apart from the ridiculous 'Tiddles' he really had no idea what a cat was supposed to be called. He had at least managed to ascertain its sex, for a cat-loving customer had identified it as a young tom, probably a few months short of a year old, but that proved of no immediate help in deciding on a name.

As is so often the case, the answer came when he had given up trying and was least expecting it. He was reclining on the settee reading a Penguin edition of *The Last Days of Socrates* when he happened to glance across at the kitten sitting motionless in the middle of the floor, apparently transfixed by nothing in particular.

'What's up with you, Socrates?' he asked, without thinking.

Having just read how the eponymous hero was inclined to go into a cataleptic trance when musing on some great metaphysical conundrum or other, he had subconsciously made a connection between the two, and that, as it happens, is how Socrates the cat came to get his name.

Socrates the cat may not have been as conversationally gifted as his namesake, but he nevertheless proved to be a good and faithful companion to the bookseller. Over the course of time they got to know each other's little ways and idiosyncrasies and gradually fell into a familiar daily routine together. Daytime was spent in the shop where Socrates would drift in and out through the store door or windows. When the sun was out, he would most often be found occupying a spot in the window. Customers would make a 'pish-wish-wish' noise to attract his attention, and at times he would deign to look up, apathetically, as if to say 'Why are you bothering me?' then promptly return to sleep. Only when he heard Truelove call did he truly sit up and take notice, and he got to understand the general nature of each communication from the tone of the bookseller's voice.

After tea they would leave through the yard and go for an early evening constitutional around the adjacent residential block, stopping at the corner shop for Truelove to buy his tobacco, newspaper, and food for them both. Socrates would jump onto walls and dart in and out of gardens as the moment required, always on the alert for perceived danger. Sometimes he would disappear from view only to pop out ahead of Truelove further along the route, and at other times he would come galloping up from behind when the bookseller called him. When back in the yard, Truelove would bolt the gate behind them and the two would retire upstairs for the evening.

At night, after a ritual of purring, butting and kneading, Socrates would habitually nuzzle his way beneath the blankets and tuck himself under the bookseller's arm or behind the crook of his knees. If he got too warm he would crawl back out and settle on top of the bed, or occasionally make his way down to the sitting room to curl up on the green settee.

The bookseller's affection for his little companion naturally deepened over time and he came to appreciate how empty his life had been without him. He was also keenly aware that had he put that bin out either one minute earlier or later, then Socrates the cat may never have been Socrates the cat.

Chapter VI

The Waitress

AFTER several months the bookseller's enthusiasm for recording the minutiae of each day evidently began to wane, and the entries got steadily fewer and farther between until eventually only the most significant events were recorded. When he read a particularly interesting book, bought in a good collection, or had a memorable encounter with a customer, for example, he made the effort to write it down, but otherwise the journal was largely neglected for some considerable time. For almost fifteen years nothing of great import happened in his very ordinary life, and during all that time he had had no communication with either the owner or staff of the café next door, except for an occasional nod or polite greeting on the pavement outside the adjoining premises.

Then, shortly after lunchtime one day, a waitress that he had never seen before, a petite and rather pretty brunette, came into his shop and began to look around. Her hair was cut in pageboy style and there was a sexual appeal about her that even the staid brown dress, white apron, and sensible shoes of the café uniform could not suppress.

The Waitress

Finding the paperback romance section, she spent some time plucking out different books, reading the back-cover blurbs, and then replacing them on the shelves.

Popular paperback novels, such as romances, thrillers, war stories, westerns, and crime, were what Truelove referred to as the 'bread and butter' books of the trade. These were the ones that brought in the core revenue of his business and put food on the table at the end of the day. Without them he would struggle to survive, so he did not disdain them. Besides, he knew many of them to be of considerable merit.

However, he was aware of others in his trade who scorned virtually all but the 'classics' in literature, failing to appreciate that the classics of today were often the popular bodice rippers and cliffhangers of the past. The best of Charles Dickens' novels started life as suspense-inducing serialisations, sold through magazines or in monthly parts bound in cheap paper wrappers. They were all about thrills and spills and mass distribution, and it is not unreasonable to suppose that there were booksellers then who considered it beneath their dignity to sell the works of Dickens.

The type of second-hand bookseller who would have nothing in the shop under a certain price, age or prestige, and who enjoyed pontificating at length on the merits of some great work of literature or other to customers with clipped accents, drew nothing but contempt from

Truelove. They were generally people who had retired from another profession and already had money behind them, and he doubted that had they to eke out a living from the books alone any of them would still be in the trade, or even have entered it in the first place. They were not genuine booksellers as far as he was concerned, nor even booklovers, but pretentious egotists who were more interested in the intellectual credibility that the association with bookselling might lend them, rather than in the books themselves.

Truelove stocked a broad cross-section of material from the very rare and expensive to the most common and cheap books that he displayed on the trestle table outside his shop. There was always a percentage of the stock that reflected his own taste, and he liked to think that in some small degree he might be influencing the world as a purveyor of knowledge. But most titles and authors he would buy in simply because they were fashionable and sure to sell quickly. That was common sense. He had to give people what they wanted, even if the books were of no personal interest, otherwise he would soon be out of business. This didn't trouble him unduly because the fundamental point was that his customers were reading *something*, no matter what. Better to read something than nothing at all, he believed, because reading *something* always allowed for the possibility of developing finer tastes.

The Waitress

After browsing the romance section for ten minutes or so, the pretty young waitress approached the desk and handed Truelove two books. He opened each in turn and added the prices that were marked inside.

'Three fifty,' he informed her.

In the brief moment that he looked up and saw her face at close quarters for the first time, he was struck by what beautifully angry and tempestuous brown eyes she had.

The waitress produced a five pound note from her dress pocket and handed it to him. When she had received her change, and the books were delivered back to her in a bag, she responded with a routine 'Thank you', then left.

She returned the following week with the same two books in her hand and asked:

'Do you do exchanges?'

'Half back on what you return against what you take out,' he explained concisely.

Apart from him stating how much she owed in the exchange, and her thanking him as a matter of course, that was the sum total of their conversation that day; and, indeed, it wasn't any more expansive on her subsequent visits, for Angie was destined to become a regular customer. Truelove knew her name from the tag she wore on the breast of her uniform. This practice, almost certainly an import from America, whereby waitresses and shop assistants had to display their first names for all and sundry to see, seemed to have spread like a contagious disease around the retail sector in recent years. Truelove regarded it as somewhat demeaning and personally intrusive, and it was something he resented on behalf of those who were forced to wear these badges. Moreover, he viewed it as a further step away from that genteel formality that he remembered so fondly from his youth, towards a coarse familiarity that he believed would only diminish respect and breed contempt. But he was willing to concede that perhaps he had simply become the archetypal grumpy and intolerant middle-aged man who had failed to move with the times.

Angie usually called in once a week to exchange a couple of paperbacks and would generally stick to romance unless that section had become moribund through a lack of fresh titles coming in. At such times she would switch to selecting crime novels or, once in a while, a thriller. There was one notable departure from this pattern, and that was when she bought a relatively expensive half-leather bound Folio Society edition of *Wuthering Heights*. Truelove noted that this was never exchanged. In Angie he thought he saw a smoulderingly wild and passionate nature not unlike that of Catherine Earnshaw, the novel's heroine, but one that appeared to have been tempered through time. He suspected that she had been attracted, like the proverbial moth to a flame, to the type of men whose lives burn most dangerously bright, and that through bitter experience had developed a hard front to the world. She was probably still only in her mid-twenties but, as with so many young women of spirit, had perhaps lived so fast and furiously in her relationships that she had learned early to be wary and suspicious of people in general, and of men in particular.

Although there was scarcely any discourse between the two, the bookseller and the waitress seemed to develop a tacit understanding and empathy for each other, even a mutual esteem. Truelove didn't readily take to overly effusive people, finding them generally intellectually vacuous and annoying. Those casual visitors who waxed most lyrical about his shop and asked the greatest number of questions tended not to buy anything at all. Where the bookseller discerned that a person had undergone a degree of physical or emotional suffering, he found that he or she was inclined to be more circumspect and insightful about life, often more genuinely considerate too, and that is why he liked Angie. He sensed that deep down she wasn't naturally cynical, but merely cautiously undemonstrative, and she did not, thankfully, fuss nauseatingly over Socrates in the way that some female customers would do.

There is no doubt that Truelove looked favourably upon Angie because of her disposition and demeanour, but at the same time it was patently obvious to him that she wasn't happy in her condition of mistrustfulness, and that was reflected in those fierce brown eyes of hers. They would only ever soften, he thought, when she found someone in whom she could truly place her trust.

Chapter VII

The Past

TRUELOVE was not yet a year old when he was pulled from the wreckage of his home during the London Blitz of 1940. Both his parents were killed in the raid and either no living relatives could be found or none were willing or able to take on the responsibility of a baby during wartime, so he was taken into care. He arrived at the local orphanage shortly after the war had ended.

In his journal he did not refer to the past, as though life before bookselling had never existed, and it was only through later investigation that I was able to glean snippets of information concerning his earlier years.

There was one exception to his silence concerning his previous existence, but that was written more in reminiscence of someone else than about himself, and it was noticeable that he made no mention of his own circumstances at the time. All he said was that as an older boy he would be given a small allowance and was permitted to go unaccompanied into the town to spend it.

When most other boys were spending their pocket money on sweets, comics, and toys, he had stumbled across a rather shabby and dilapidated double-fronted bookshop in a quiet little side-street. The windows were crammed to the top with a chaotic jumble of volumes, so that all passers-by could see was a disorderly wall of edges and odd angles of books pressed hard against the glass. There was a little recess in the middle of the two windows that led to the front door, and a broken bell gave a hollow clunk as one entered. Apart from a small rectangular area in the centre, the floor space was taken up with solid piles of books, so deep and so high that it was impossible to reach the books on the visible parts of the shelves without leaning and stretching awkwardly over. Volumes on the higher shelves were rendered entirely inaccessible. The shop was pervaded by that type of fusty smell peculiar to books that have been stored in cold and damp conditions, and only the most ardent of booklovers would be prepared to tolerate it in search of a hidden gem.

The bookseller's desk was entirely buried beneath a mountain of books too, and only by intuition would one know that it was there at all. One side of it completely merged into the wall and on the other side was a narrow pathway between the books that would just about allow access to and from its rear, with some careful sideways shuffling. No attempt had been made to place the stock in any sort of order and it might easily have been inferred from the whole shambolic presentation that the selling of books was of much less importance than their accumulation, and perhaps merely a necessary evil.

The first time that Truelove entered the shop he could see no sign of anyone in attendance. He had stood for a moment or two not knowing how to proceed, when suddenly the shopkeeper craned his neck in curiosity and appeared to the boy as a disembodied head above the mass of books stacked on his desk. He was an odd, gaunt looking creature, this bookseller, with snowy stubble on his face, and long, straggly white hair, streaked with yellow. He had a hooked nose, set between two beady little black eyes, and looked for all the world like a bird of prey. Having established the nature of the intruder with a cursory glance, the old man gave a short, contemptuous grunt before disappearing from view again.

The young Truelove took this as an indication that whereas he may not have been particularly welcome on the premises, he was at least being given permission to stay under sufferance. Initially he just stood with his hands clasped behind his back, slowly turning his head to take in his surroundings. Then he became a little more adventurous and began tentatively handling a few of the books on the top of the piles, glancing towards the desk now and then to see if he was being watched. But, gradually, he grew more and more absorbed in his serendipitous search until his inhibitions and fear of censure were entirely forgotten, and he started to steadily dismantle the heaps of books around him. It was like being in the middle of a giant lucky-dip, only better, because here he could put back what he didn't like and choose what he wanted to keep. When he finally decided upon something that fully satisfied him, and regained a sense of where he was, he realised that he'd immured himself in the middle of a wall of books and had to quickly re-stack his way out of it before his handiwork was discovered. Then he positioned himself in front of the hidden desk with the book in his hand.

'Excuse me,' he said timidly.

There was no response.

He summoned up his courage.

'Excuse me!' he repeated, only this time so loudly as to almost startle himself.

'Yes! What do you want?' came the fierce rejoinder.

'I'd like to buy this book, please.'

There was a short pause before the old man's head popped back up. This time he took a moment to carefully eye his customer up and down.

'Where did you find that?' he demanded.

Truelove pointed.

'Humph! That had no business being there!' he announced quite enigmatically. 'Take it away, boy!' he ordered with a dismissive wave of the hand, 'Just take it away!'

Then he vanished behind his book mountain again.

Truelove stood motionless for a while, not quite knowing what had just happened or what to do next. Then he made his way over to one of the reassembled stacks and recovered another book that he'd toyed with buying.

'Excuse me,' he said, standing before the desk again, 'May I buy this?'

When the bookseller reappeared, Truelove held the book out to him. The old man hesitated before taking it, then checked the price inside and said more softly:

'Two shillings.'

The boy gave him half a crown and waited as the old chap rattled through a tin of coins in search of the sixpence change. This was duly handed over and Truelove left the shop in a state of euphoria with his two books.

Although he came away bemused and a little afraid of the old bookseller it didn't deter him from revisiting the shop; but, on the next occasion that he bought a book, he noticed that the shopkeeper had given him too much change, and he made the mistake of telling him so.

'Are you questioning my ability to calculate, boy?' the old man barked indignantly.

'No, sir!'

'Right then, be off with you!'

From then on Truelove handed the money over and accepted whatever change he was given, which was always wrong, although noticeably never to his disadvantage.

Every Saturday for more than a year Truelove religiously made his way to the bookshop with his allowance and errand money in his pocket, and delighted in exploring the thousands of jumbled volumes. His excitement was always heightened when he discovered fresh stock scattered among the chaos.

Then, one day, he arrived to find the shop closed. He tried the door several times before finally accepting that it was locked. He peered in through the glass panel but failed to catch a glimpse of the bookseller. For more than an hour he paced up and down on the pavement outside, periodically looking through the door for signs of life, but there were none. Eventually he was forced to give up and left with a very heavy heart indeed.

The following Saturday seemed to take an eternity to come, but he raced down to the bookshop only to be faced by the same disappointment. For the next several weeks he continued to return in the hope that he would find the shop open again, but it never was. Even when after several months he arrived to discover the windows had been whitewashed he still, in his boyhood innocence and optimism, did not entirely despair. It was not until he stood on the far side of the street and looked across to see trays of vegetables displayed outside, and a bright new greengrocer's sign above the door, that the devastating truth finally hit him. His beloved bookshop was gone forever.

The catalyst for the recording of these memories in his journal was the offer of a copy of the very same book that the old man had given him on his first visit — a handsomely illustrated Collins edition of *Treasure Island* and *Kidnapped* combined, which had seemed so enormous to him at the time. It was only on reflection as an adult that he came to appreciate the kindness of that cranky old bookseller and how he had tried to disguise it behind rude irascibility. Truelove was sure that the old bird-like bookman had deduced his circumstances from the very start.

Chapter VIII

The Silk Bookmark

O N a quiet Monday morning, Truelove had become engrossed in re-reading an old favourite when he heard the doorbell tinkle. There had evidently been no refurbishment of the shop during his tenure, almost certainly because he hadn't the funds at the time of buying it, and later because the upheaval of removing the books and shelves would have proved much too onerous. But he did invest in a new bell. It alerted him to the fact that somebody was coming in, although he was not in the habit of looking up whenever he heard it. That would mean greeting his customers and the exchange of tedious pleasantries, something he wished to avoid at all costs. So, for a minute or two, he was unaware of the nature of his latest visitor. It was on catching the scent of a particularly appealing perfume that curiosity got the better of him, and he glanced up to see a most stunningly attractive woman, of early middle age, standing in front of the shelves. She was so attractive, in fact, that he felt decidedly nervous and uncomfortable in her presence, and buried his head in his book again, waiting for her to leave. Female beauty intimidated him, although it wasn't a problem that he faced too often. Attractive women weren't a common sight within the confines of his shop, Angie being one of the rare exceptions. He had a theory that good-looking people generally preferred to furnish their bodies rather than their minds, and he often wondered if proper scientific study would bear that out.

After scanning the words on the page in front of him several times over, but taking nothing in, his pretend reading was interrupted by what he most dreaded and yet secretly desired at the same time.

'Excuse me. I wonder if you could help.'

The voice was soft and mellifluous, and instilled him with utter terror. He looked up in her direction, but not daring to meet her eyes.

'I haven't got time to browse properly today,' she explained. 'Perhaps you could recommend something?'

'I don't do that,' replied Truelove more brusquely than he intended.

The woman was visibly hurt and embarrassed.

'Oh, I see,' she said. 'I'm sorry.'

She stood awkwardly for a moment, as though temporarily stunned, then made her way towards the door. As she was in the process of closing it behind her, Truelove, feeling ashamed of his rudeness, and not by nature wanting to hurt anyone's feelings, suddenly called out:

'But there is this!'

He held up his copy of *The Bankrupt Bookseller*.

She looked round, hesitated for a moment, then gave a forgiving smile and made her way elegantly towards him. He could not bring himself to make eye contact as he passed the book over, but observed her exquisitely feminine hands as she took and examined it.

'I'm not sure that you would like it,' he said. 'It wouldn't be everyone's cup of tea.'

'No, not at all,' she replied reassuringly. 'It would be most appropriate. My father was a keen book collector and used to take me on his expeditions around the second-hand bookshops when I was a girl, so I should feel quite at home with this.'

Nonetheless, he suspected that she had said it merely out of politeness.

'But you are reading it?'

'I've read it before and have other copies, so …'

'Then how much do I owe you?' she asked, opening her handbag and reaching inside for her purse.

Truelove held up his hand and shook his head.

'I couldn't charge you,' he said. 'You might not even like it. Just borrow it and bring it back when you are ready.'

'Are you sure?'

'Yes,' said Truelove.

'Well, then, I promise I'll take good care of it — and thank you!'

By this stage Socrates had made his way in from the store and had stationed himself at her feet, looking searchingly up at her.

'Oh, hello! Who's this?' she asked, crouching down to pet him. The bookseller couldn't help but notice the perfect shapeliness of her bare legs as her skirt rode above the knees.

'He's called Socrates.'

'Well, Socrates, aren't you the handsome chap? And what a fine name you have too!'

The cat was unusually sociable and seemed to enjoy the attention for once. In all the fifteen years that he had been in the shop he had never before appeared so amenable to being petted by a customer. She stroked him and scratched his neck for a while before tantalizingly drawing back her hair with her hands and getting to her feet again.

'Anyway, thank you once more for lending me the book. But I really need to be going now.'

The bookseller nodded.

'Goodbye, Mr Truelove,' she said, adding, 'It is Mr Truelove, isn't it?'

'Yes, Truelove by name, but not in practice,' he answered in a feeble attempt at a joke.

She smiled anyway.

'And goodbye to you too, Socrates. I'll see you again soon.'

She paused at the doorway.

'Oh, I'm Elizabeth Grayson, by the way — Beth,' she said.

Then she disappeared into the street.

Truelove sincerely wished that they would see her again, and not for the sake of having his book returned. That was an insignificant price to pay for having had this beautiful woman in his life, if only ever for a few minutes.

For the next couple of days he constantly replayed the scene in his mind, recalling every word she had spoken and each little detail of her that he had glimpsed, from the silky, shoulder-length raven hair that framed those piercing blue eyes, to her perfectly manicured and varnished fingernails. She was the epitome of femininity in his eyes.

By Thursday he thought it possible that she could have finished the book and might walk through the door at any moment, so his level of anticipation grew with the passing hours, but she did not come. Neither did she appear on the Friday or Saturday. Sunday seemed to drag interminably and he had never before been so keen to get the shop opened on a Monday morning. He was up at the crack of dawn, impatient for the time to come when he could unlock the door to begin another week of business. For only when the shop was open was there the chance that he might see her again.

But, as each day of the new week passed, and there

was still no sign of her, his hopes began to fade, and he eventually began to resign himself to the likelihood that she might not be back. He hadn't deceived himself into believing that such a woman could possibly have an interest in him, but he was nevertheless eager for a few more short minutes in her company. He also knew that his longing to see her was entirely irrational, based on little more than appearance, for which she could take no credit. She had a most agreeable personality, certainly, but then many of his other female customers were equally pleasant, and yet he had not felt the same way about them. The primeval force of nature that is physical attraction, he concluded, is an irresistible enemy, and one that could not be defeated by reason, no matter how hard one tried.

It was between the pages of the journal in which this encounter was described that Truelove had placed the silk bookmark.

* * * * * * * * * *

Not long after Beth's visit parcels began to arrive mysteriously at the door to the flat. Truelove came downstairs one morning to discover a plastic bag lying beside his daily bottle of milk. It had a sticky label with 'Socrates' written on it. He went back into the hallway and opened it. Inside, wrapped in greaseproof paper, was strip of boneless salmon.

'It seems that you have an admirer, Socrates,' he said, when back upstairs. 'You'll eat well today.'

But that was not the end of it. The packages kept appearing periodically, though to no set pattern, except never on a Sunday. Sometimes they contained salmon, and at other times cod and other varieties of fish. He could not imagine for the life of him who was behind this largesse. When the milkman came round to collect his money one Thursday evening, Truelove asked him if he had seen anything and could shed some light on the matter, but the milkman just shrugged his shoulders.

After a while he gave up trying to guess who was leaving these gifts and thought no more about it. Then, one morning, when he happened to be up and about particularly early, he opened the door to find yet another delivery of fish on the step. Hearing a rumbling noise off to his right, he turned his head just in time to see Christmas Eve and her trolley disappearing round the corner of the block.

Chapter IX

Great Expectations

I⸏ᴛ seems to be a law of nature that the more desperate one is to see somebody the less likely that person is to appear. Truelove eagerly awaited Beth's return for more than a fortnight before he finally began to resign himself to not seeing her again. During that period he had uncharacteristically glanced up in anticipation when the shop bell tinkled, each time hoping that it would be Beth whom he would see walking through the door. Whenever the shop was empty he would step outside and look up and down the street in the vain hope that he might see her heading his way. But, of course, she didn't come.

Naturally, Truelove's high level of anticipation could not be sustained indefinitely, and into the third week since she had visited the shop he subconsciously decided that she would not be back. The short encounter between them had left an indelible mark on his mind, so he would never entirely forget her, but he had to accept the experience for what it was and move on. He reprimanded himself for having been so foolish as to make more of it in his mind than it merited, and was annoyed that he had let his emotions rule his head in that way. How, he wondered, had he allowed himself to behave like a schoolboy with a crush?

But the obverse of that law of nature is that the object of desire invariably turns up when least expected, and when one's mind is otherwise occupied. Beth's reappearance was no exception to the rule. The bookseller had placed the whole episode into the furthest recesses of his mind and had just got back on an even emotional keel when she entered his life for the second time.

On the Friday of that third week he was in the process of serving a customer when he heard someone entering the shop. His view of the door was obscured, so he wasn't immediately aware that it was her, but the memorable scent of her perfume alerted him to the possibility of her presence. When the customer moved away from the desk to make his exit, Truelove saw that it was indeed Beth, standing in the background, waiting.

Despite the change in attire, and the fact that she was wearing sunglasses, she was instantly recognisable to him. He thought it slightly odd that she should wear sunglasses on a dull October afternoon, but for all he knew that was what the fashionable and chic did. Such matters were beyond his knowledge and comprehension.

When she saw that the bookseller was free she smiled and made her way over to him, reaching into her bag as she came. She produced *The Bankrupt Bookseller* and handed it across the desk to him.

'I really, really enjoyed that. Thank you!' she said. 'And I'm sorry it took me so long to return it, but I got caught up with one thing and another.'

'I'm glad you liked it,' replied Truelove, for want of anything else to say.

'It really was amusing, yet sad at the same time. The poor bookseller never stood a chance, did he?'

Truelove attempted a smile.

'You see,' she added positively, 'recommending a book isn't always a bad thing, is it?'

Once again Socrates ambled on to the scene and sat himself down at her feet, much to Truelove's surprise. He couldn't imagine why the old cat had made a beeline for Beth on both occasions when he was generally in the habit of ignoring customers. He wondered what on earth it could be about her that attracted Socrates' attention. Was it some sort of psychic connection, or something much more prosaic, like the smell of her perfume or a type of pheromone she emitted? Whatever the reason, there was no doubt that Socrates, like his master, had taken a liking to her.

'Well, if it isn't my friend, Socrates!' she declared.

'You remembered his name,' Truelove remarked.

'Why, of course! It's hardly an easy one to forget.'

As she kneeled down and turned her head towards Socrates, Truelove saw that she had bruising around the side of her eye, and an instant and uncontrollable anger welled up inside him.

'Who did that!?' he demanded.

The words were out before he knew it, and took him as much by surprise as her.

Beth got back to her feet.

'Who did what?' she asked sharply, but knowing full well what he meant.

Truelove was still too shocked by his involuntary outburst to respond. He just stood in silence, staring at her despondently.

'Well, thank you again for lending me the book, Mr Truelove,' said Beth in a very curt and formal manner. Then she turned abruptly and left the shop.

The bookseller was devastated. For weeks he had longed to have contact with this beautiful woman again. He had imagined different scenarios as to how it would be, and had rehearsed what he might say in each situation, but not for a moment did he consider that it could end in any way badly. In reality, the outcome could hardly have been worse. Now the pleasant memories and imaginings were supplanted by the re-enactment of this distasteful last encounter, which seemed to play on a permanent loop within his mind.

The thought of a man inflicting harm on any woman would have been enough to enrage him, but to mar beauty somehow exacerbated the crime, and his reason had been temporarily overwhelmed by passion. He had automatically jumped to the conclusion that a husband or boyfriend was the culprit and, on reflection, her reaction confirmed him in this opinion. If the bruising had been the result of a mere accident then surely she would just have laughed his question off and explained his mistake? But she didn't. She was angry, and he had heard of women who would vehemently protect abusive partners from censure, no matter what. But he nevertheless cursed himself for his forwardness and lack of control. If he'd only kept his head, he thought, then she might have come back, and perhaps he'd even have got the chance to help her in some way. As it was, he was convinced that she was gone for good.

Chapter X

The Return

WHEN memories are painful the human mind works hard to suppress them, but the process invariably takes time. In Truelove's case it took several days to force the incident with Beth to the back of his mind and for his emotions to resume a familiar and comfortable equilibrium. Occasionally something would trigger a fleeting recollection of the unfortunate episode but, after a few weeks had passed, he generally thought no more of it, or of Beth. His focus and consideration returned entirely to the bookselling business and, of course, his faithful feline companion. Socrates now did little more than sleep most of the day, but he continued to accompany the bookseller on his evening constitutionals, come rain or shine.

The shop was well-stocked and doing a brisk trade. The town had been expanding for some years. New housing developments had been built and the population was soaring. The commercial outlets naturally benefited from this, and the bookshop was no exception. Truelove was busier than ever, but there were still quiet periods during the day nonetheless, and he often used those hours to trawl through the 'wants' ads in the second-hand book trade magazines. Book businesses offering a search service to their customers would list the titles that they required in these publications. Truelove, more to occupy his time than through necessity, responded to the advertisements and quoted the details and prices of any matching titles that he had in stock. Every week he would post off a batch of quotation slips to various dealers around the country. Most often, a bookseller who replied would write 'Please send' on the slip and return it with a cheque in payment. Truelove would then securely wrap whatever books were ordered and take the parcels to the Post Office before opening the shop in the morning.

It was during one of those quiet spells when he was busy filling in quotation slips that the bell alerted him to someone entering the shop; but, as usual, he carried on regardless. It was several minutes before he caught the scent of that familiar perfume once again. He looked up expectantly from his task. Momentarily, he felt as though his heart had stopped beating. For there, sure enough — standing with a book in her hand — was Beth. She gave him a nervous smile, and then tentatively approached the desk.

Holding up a paperback copy of *Under the Greenwood Tree,* she said, with a feigned breeziness:

'I've been meaning to get this for a long time. It's the only Hardy novel I haven't read.'

The bookseller was still too disoriented to respond, so

she filled the void, but in a distinctly more solemn tone.

'I really do hope I didn't offend you last time — stupid thing to say — of course I did — storming off like that.'

'It's okay,' said Truelove softly.

'No, it's not okay. I was under a lot of strain at the time, but that's no excuse for my behaviour. You were only showing concern.'

There was a short pause, and then Beth resumed:

'Look, let me make it up to you. Can I take you next door for a cup of coffee, perhaps?'

'Well — I —'

Truelove was caught completely off guard by the suggestion and for an instant he didn't know how to react. This was taking him right out of his comfort zone. He desperately wanted to go with her but, at the same time, the thought panicked him. He had little concept of how to socialise, especially with a woman, and he feared being rejected for his dullness. Moreover, he was embarrassed by the shabbiness of his appearance. He did not want her to see the holes in his jacket elbows and the worn sheen on his trouser knees. What would she think? Behind his desk he felt safe and immune from scrutiny. Did he really wish to expose himself to the risk of disapproval and repudiation?

'I'm sorry,' she said. 'Have I put you in an awkward position?'

Truelove glimpsed the anxious look on her face.

'No, no!' he replied decidedly. 'It's quiet. I'll lock up.'
Despite his reservations the bookseller was not prepared
to risk offending her for the sake of his own insecurities.

Chapter XI

Playing Truant

I T was on the very rarest of occasions, and only through absolute necessity, that the bookseller had previously closed the shop during business hours. There was an element of guilt involved in locking up merely to go to a café and engage in chit-chat, and yet it made him feel strangely liberated at the same time. It gave him a buzz somewhat akin to that of the schoolboy truant. This was the bookseller living life on the edge.

As they sat down, Beth began to apologise again for how she had reacted on her last visit.

'That day,' she said, 'I was at a low ebb. I was tired, emotional and, quite frankly, embarrassed. So, when you asked …'

'It wasn't my place to say anything,' Truelove interjected.

She dismissed his remark with a wave of her hand.

'You were concerned, and bless you for that! I had no right to be cross with you.'

'Anyway,' she continued, 'you assumed that I'd been struck — and you were right. It was …'

She broke off when the waitress, who happened to be

Angie, came across to take their order. Angie stood beside the table with her pen poised over her notepad, and looked first to Beth and then to Truelove. Her face betrayed not the slightest sign of recognition or surprise at seeing him in the café. It was as if it was a regular occurrence or the two were perfect strangers.

Beth looked to Truelove for confirmation.

'Coffee?' she asked.

He nodded.

'Just two coffees, please,' she said, giving Angie a friendly smile.

Angie quickly scribbled on her pad and then disappeared without saying a word. Beth waited a moment and checked that they couldn't be overheard.

'It was my mother,' she announced in a low voice.

'What was?' asked Truelove.

'It was Mum who hit me.'

Truelove was taken aback.

'Your mother?'

'Yes. But it's not what you think,' she assured him. 'She has Alzheimer's, you see — and sometimes she gets very confused and angry, and just strikes out. It's not her fault, poor thing. She has no idea what she's doing.'

Beth expanded on the situation at home and it was quite apparent to Truelove that caring for someone with dementia was no easy job. He admired her fortitude and dedication, but didn't like to think of her having to cope on her own.

'Does your husband not help?'

'I'm not married — I came close a couple of times, but it wasn't to be — anyway, that's another story; but, in terms of help, Dorothy next door is a godsend. She'll come in whenever she can to give me a break for a few hours. Then I can get away to do some shopping, or get my hair done, or even indulge myself in a visit to the lovely bookshop!'

'What about you?' Beth asked. 'Is there a Mrs Truelove?'

The bookseller smiled ironically.

'I am much too odd for anyone to put up with.'

'I'm sure that's not true. But don't you ever get lonely?' she asked.

'I don't know.'

Beth was puzzled.

'You don't know?'

'Life is the way it's always been, and I suppose I can't miss what I've never had.'

'But at least you have Socrates,' she suggested.

'Yes, I have Socrates.'

'By the way, what is *your* name — your Christian name, that is? Calling you Mr Truelove sounds so formal.'

'Giles,' he replied diffidently.

'Why, that's a lovely name!' said Beth, 'And it suits you. It has a scholarly, gentlemanly ring about it.'

She extended her hand.

'Pleased to meet you, Giles! I'm Beth, in case you've forgotten.'

Truelove shyly clasped her delicate white hand in his. It was a self-conscious moment of pure elation for him.

The coffee arrived, and they continued to chat quite freely about this subject and that. The bookseller, whilst still not perfectly at ease, found that he was enjoying her company immensely, and was positively loquacious by his standards.

Beth told him that she had been a model for several years, doing mostly catalogue work, but gave it up to assist her father in his promotions business. He died not long after her mother's condition was diagnosed, and they decided to sell their house in London and move back to the town where her mother had been born and bred. They had been back just under a year, during which time her mother's condition had deteriorated rapidly.

'If there's ever anything I can do to help, anything at all …' Truelove volunteered.

'It's fine, honestly. I didn't mean to burden you with my troubles. But thank you for the kind offer.'

She checked her watch.

'I suppose I'd better be on my way now.'

When Angie came with the bill Truelove attempted to pay it, but Beth was insistent.

'This is my treat — by way of apology.'

As they stood on the street outside the café Beth sudden-ly remembered that she hadn't paid Truelove for the copy of *Under the Greenwood Tree*. She fumbled around in her purse, pulled out the right change, and held it out to him.

'No,' he said firmly. 'There was really nothing to apol-ogise for — so that is my treat.'

'Thank you, Giles. You are a kind man, and I really enjoyed your company today. I do hope that we can do it again some time.'

With that she turned and made her way briskly towards her bus stop on the main street.

Truelove stood and watched until she disappeared around the corner. He could scarcely believe what had just happened.

Chapter XII

A Request

Giles Truelove was the archetypal nondescript man. He was of average height, build and weight, and had mousy brown hair and hazel eyes. He was neither ugly, nor handsome, and had no particularly distinguishing features. Physically, he was the ordinary man personified. He was well aware that he was no matinee idol, and in Beth's company he had felt somewhat fraudulent, as though he had no business being with her at all. So he did not believe for a moment that the relationship would blossom into some sort of passionate romance. Nevertheless, he instinctively began to take more care of his appearance and invested in some new clothes. He started to shave every day instead of every two or three days, and not for a very long time had he paid so much attention to his personal presentation.

During the next several months Beth would generally come to the bookshop once a week, although sometimes the interval might stretch further. The most important thing for Truelove was to know that she would always return at some point. If the shop was quiet, and she wasn't in a rush, then they normally went to the café for a cup of coffee and a chat, otherwise the conversations were conducted across the bookseller's desk, between customers.

The subject of conversation was wide and varied, but most often they would discuss books that they'd both read, or the trials and tribulations of bookselling, or talk about the situation at home with her mother. Sometimes she would proffer bits of information on her past life, but there was never any voluntary reciprocation. If she asked him about his past, then he would answer, but without elaboration, and she didn't press him.

The friendship between them naturally developed and matured over time, but the backdrop did not vary beyond the café or the bookshop. That is, not until one Saturday afternoon, when out of the blue, she asked him:

'Will you come to church with me on Sunday?'

He reflected for a moment.

'In all conscience, I couldn't.'

'Why? Don't you believe in God?'

'I don't know.'

'You don't know whether you believe in God or not?'

'Much greater minds than mine have battled with that question and failed to find a definitive answer,' said Truelove. 'But,' he continued, 'even if I did believe in God, I would still struggle with the concept of Christianity — or, for that matter — any other religion that relies on "sacred" text as a fundamental basis of belief. If God does exist — and he wanted to communicate with us — I doubt that he'd choose to do it through intermediaries or use such an imperfect medium as the printed word.'

'Well, this will make me sound very foolish, but I've never really thought too deeply about it all,' Beth confessed. 'I suppose I've more or less just accepted at face value what I was brought up to believe. But all I can say is that I find comfort in those monotonous Sunday sermons, the Bible readings, the familiar hymns, and the whole rite and ritual of the church. At the end of the day, maybe I *am* deceiving myself, but I'm happy in my delusion.'

'If you find solace in it, then who am I to deny you that? And I must admit that even I have a soft spot for the Bible. The authorized King James Version is — if nothing else — one of the richest and most beautiful pieces of literature ever written. I understand perfectly how seductive it can be.'

'But whether I'm right or wrong to follow my faith as I do,' Beth resumed, 'I am still convinced in my heart that there's something more — something beyond this life.'

'I couldn't honestly say that you are mistaken in your conviction,' the bookseller responded. 'And I sincerely hope that I haven't offended you by what I have said — or by declining your invitation? You know that I would never …'

'Well, I can hardly be angry with you for not wanting

to be a hypocrite, can I? But will you at least meet me *after* church tomorrow? I have something important to ask you.'

'I will, of course,' said Truelove.

Chapter XIII

The Book Collection

AT the appointed hour the bookseller waited outside the church, pacing up and down on the opposite side of the road. As the congregation came out after the service, he saw Beth stop briefly to exchange greetings with a group of people gathered in front of the arched entrance, before making her way down the path and through the churchyard gate. She was dressed in a smart navy blue trouser suit and looked as elegant as ever.

She greeted Truelove with a warm smile.

'It's a beautiful May morning, and I have my sensible shoes on — let's walk!' she suggested.

They strolled for about half a mile before turning into the narrow, winding, tree-lined road that led to the neighbouring village, exchanging a few desultory remarks as they went. As they approached the picturesque village, with its little thatched cottages and small boats bobbing in the harbour, Beth stopped where the coastal path that led back to the town began.

'Shall we head back this way?'

The track was too narrow to walk two abreast, so Beth led the way. They had proceeded in silence for perhaps ten minutes, when Beth suddenly announced over her shoulder:

'My mother's in a nursing home.'

'Oh?'

'Yes — since Monday. She got really bad recently, and I just couldn't cope anymore. I had to watch her constantly, and she was getting more and more violent. I couldn't even have Dorothy in to give me a break, because it was too much to ask of her.'

'I'm sorry to hear that,' said Truelove, 'truly sorry.'

'I feel so ashamed — so guilty — but I don't know what else I could have done. If I'd carried on, my own health was in danger — and if anything happened to me there'd be nobody to look after her welfare.'

She stopped and turned to face him.

'You once said that if there was ever anything that you could do for me?'

'Yes.'

'Did you mean it?'

'Of course I did.'

'Well, there *is* something that you could do for me now. But it's a big favour to ask, and I will understand perfectly if you don't want to do it.'

'What is it?' he asked.

'I'd like you to dispose of my father's books for me — in the best way you see fit.'

'I see.'

'I really have no other option. I have enough money to cover one or two months of Mum's care fees, but after that, well… If the house has to be sold then I'm homeless — it's in her name, you see — and I'd struggle to find the rent for somewhere else. I've no idea how much the books are worth, but they might buy me some time at least.'

'We'll see soon enough,' said the bookseller. 'And, please, don't worry — you'll never want for a roof over your head, or anything else for that matter, while I'm still alive.'

'Thank you, Giles,' she said, a little tremulously. 'You are so kind. I really don't know what I'd do without you right now.'

They continued along the undulating, meandering path, between rows of gorse and past sandy coves, until they reached the expanse of beach on the outskirts of the town. Midway along, between the seafront houses, was a narrow entry that led back to the road on which they had started. As they trudged along it, with rather weary legs, Truelove turned to Beth and asked:

'So when do you want me to look at the books?'

'There's no time like the present, I suppose,' she replied. 'We're not far from the house now, anyway.'

A few minutes and a couple of turns later they arrived in front of a modest red brick semi-detached house with a bay window.

'Here we are!' Beth announced.

She unlocked the door and led him straight through to the front parlour.

'The blinds are kept closed permanently to stop the books getting sunned,' she explained.

'Quite right,' said Truelove approvingly.

The books were situated on the wall directly opposite the window, displayed on hand-made wooden shelves that were varnished with a teak finish. The bookseller could tell at a glance that the collection was one of good quality. It was eclectic, but with a preponderance of travel, topography, and architecture.

'I'll leave you to it then,' said Beth, observing that the bookseller was already absorbed.

As soon as she had left the room, Truelove began his assessment in earnest. He first made a rough calculation of the total number of books on the shelves, and then started picking out particular volumes for examination.

Among the travel books was a three-volume Dublin edition of Captain James Cook's *A Voyage to the Pacific Ocean*, 1784, bound in full calf with red and black double lettering-pieces on the spine; *Glimpses of China: A Series of Vandyck Photogravures illustrating Chinese life and surroundings*, with 30 tipped-in plates by Donald Mennie, and published in Shanghai, *circa* 1920; an elephant folio of *Spain* by Baron Charles Davillier, published in 1876, and finely illustrated with full-page engravings by Gustave Doré.

There was also a number of limited editions, including a vellum-bound copy of Abbot Gasquet's *The Greater Abbeys of England,* 1908, with tipped-in colour plates by Warwick Goble. Written in pencil on the verso of the free front end-paper was a bookseller's price — £2-10-0. And on the recto of the flyleaf was printed: 'Of this Special Edition of THE GREATER ABBEYS of ENGLAND Sixty Copies have been printed, of which Fifty only are for sale. This is No. …' And the number 31 had been hand-written above the dots.

As he neared the end of his appraisal, Truelove plucked a nineteenth century copy of the King James Version of the Bible from a row of miscellaneous books to see what had been bookmarked, and it opened at the Epistle of James, where his eyes fell upon the lines from Chapter 4, Verse 14, 'Whereas ye know not what shall be on the morrow. For what is your life? It is even a vapour, that appeareth for a little time, and then vanisheth away.' The uncertainty of the future and the fleeting, ephemeral nature of life made him momentarily pensive. What would tomorrow bring for him, he wondered.

In all, there were approximately six hundred volumes, of which about one hundred, in Truelove's estimation, were of reasonable rarity. Beth's father had certainly been a man of good taste when it came to books.

Truelove had finished his estimation and was casually browsing the books for personal interest when Beth came back to check on him.

'Well, what's the verdict?' she asked.

'First, I would advise putting them to auction where you're likely to get collectors' prices, rather than selling to trade. Second — and bearing in mind that this is by no means an exact science — I would expect them to fetch somewhere between fifteen and twenty thousand pounds — perhaps a little more on a good day, but certainly no less.'

'Wow!' she exclaimed. 'I really didn't expect them to be worth that much. That should cover my mother's expenses for the best part of a year at least.'

Then she thought for a moment.

'Do you think I could possibly impose further upon your good nature?'

'Go on.'

'Well, on the little regular income we've had to live on, it wasn't so much of a problem, but I'm hopeless when it comes to budgeting and finance. If there's money sitting in my account then I just know I'll be tempted to dip into it. I'll buy a dress here, a nice pair of shoes there, and say to myself that it hardly matters; but, before I know it, a month's fees for the nursing home will have been spent. I know what I'm like.'

Truelove was as direct as ever.

'So what exactly is it that you want me to do?'

'I was wondering if — if you'd be prepared to take charge of the proceeds yourself and pay the fees for me? I know that it's putting you on the spot, but don't be afraid to say "no" if you want to. I'll understand.'

But Truelove was deeply gratified that she placed so much trust in him.

'If that's what you want me to do, then I'll do it,' he said.

He came back the following Sunday afternoon in a van that had been hired in the town. He brought in about thirty cardboard boxes that he coded with a felt marker as he packed the books away.

Beth stood silently and watched. She looked disconsolate.

'What's the matter?' he asked, catching sight of her expression as he turned to grab another empty box.

'I'm just sad to see them go, that's all. They've been with me all my life. I was there when my father bought many of them. It's like losing a bit of him all over again. But, needs must, I suppose.'

When the job was finished and final box loaded into the van, Truelove went back to the front door where Beth was standing. She held out an old silk bookmark of Victorian vintage that had a golden tassel on the end.

'Here!' she said, 'I want you to have this.'

It had an intricate floral design at the top, with 'To a

friend' printed across it on an heraldic scroll; and the verse below read:

> Of all the gifts which heaven bestows,
> There is one above all measure,
> And that's a friend midst all our woes,
> A friend is a found treasure.
> To thee I give that sacred name,
> For thou art such to me,
> And ever proudly will I claim
> To be a friend to thee.

'I know it's not much,' said Beth, 'and I know it's a little sentimental, but it seems so appropriate for you to have it.'

Chapter XIV

Empty Shelves

FIFTEEN months passed. In the meantime, Beth had found a job on the make-up counter of the local department store. Most weekdays she would call into the bookshop during her lunch hour, just to show her face and say 'hello'. It was generally the busiest part of the day for Truelove, so it wasn't convenient for him to close the shop and go off for a cup of coffee. Saturdays were a bad time too. But, occasionally, whenever Beth had time off during the week, they would prearrange a meeting in the bookshop at a suitable hour before going to the café for a proper catch-up without interruptions.

It was on one of those prearranged occasions that Beth came into the shop just as Truelove was declining to buy a box of books. When the would-be vendor left, she stepped forward to the bookseller's desk.

'No good?' she asked.

'The usual book club editions and out-of-date reference works.'

'Pity,' she said, glancing around. 'It looks as though you could do with a bit of fresh stock coming in.'

Wide gaps had developed on the shelves and the stock had never looked so depleted.

'Sometimes the supply of good books dries up for long periods,' Truelove explained. 'It's just the way it goes.'

'Well, if we're going for coffee I suppose we'd better not stay away too long — just in case you miss the offer of that once-in-a-lifetime collection!'

They waited for a solitary browser to leave and then took their opportunity to escape to the café. As soon as they got settled at a table, Beth said,

'By the way, on the subject of book collections, there can't be too much left from the sale of my father's books? I would have thought that the money must be all but gone by now.'

Truelove shifted uneasily in his seat. He had never actually told her how much was raised on the sale of her father's collection, because she had not asked. For her part, she had assumed that the figure was more or less what he'd said it would be and, if otherwise, then she'd have expected him to say so. She had trusted him implicitly and had simply left him to get on with it.

'There's enough to cover you for a while yet,' Truelove answered. 'Don't worry — I have everything in hand. When it's time to get concerned I will let you know. But, in the meantime, just leave all that to me.'

There was something in his manner and in the

evasiveness of the response that left Beth feeling a little uneasy. She began to suspect that all was not quite right — that there was something he was keeping from her; but she deferred pressing him on the matter.

The coffee arrived and the subject changed. Truelove was in the middle of telling her about a particular incident in the bookshop that morning when he spotted her wince in pain.

'What's wrong?' he asked.

'It's nothing,' she replied dismissively, 'Just a stomach cramp. I'll have eaten something that disagrees with me, that's all.'

When they got outside and were about to part, Truelove was still concerned.

'Do you want me to see you home?' he asked.

'No! Not at all — I'm fine — really!'

'Are you sure?'

'Yes, I'm sure. You get back to the shop before you miss the offer of that collection! I'll drop in to see you tomorrow.'

As it happened, he wouldn't see her again for another fortnight, and it was not to be in the most auspicious of circumstances.

Chapter XV

The Last Days of Socrates

TRUELOVE was not unduly concerned when Beth failed to appear. He simply assumed that she had succumbed to a stomach bug and had been laid low for a while, and he knew that Dorothy would be on hand to look after her, should it prove necessary. She would turn up again when she was ready. For the moment, he had a more pressing issue on his mind. Socrates had scarcely moved and barely eaten for days. He just lay motionless on the green settee from morning to night, and it had become increasingly difficult to rouse him from his lethargy.

It had been many months since Socrates had joined Truelove on his evening stroll around the block. On the last occasion he got as far as the yard gate and would go no further. Truelove had walked on to the end of the alley, looking over his shoulder as he went; but when Socrates showed no inclination to follow, the bookseller retraced his steps.

'Poor old chap!' he said, bending down to pet him. 'We'll get you back inside, eh?'

He lifted Socrates, carried him upstairs, and laid him

on the green settee. The aged cat was never to make the journey again.

From that time on, Socrates became steadily less active. When it got to the stage where he was hardly able to move at all, Truelove would make him as comfortable as possible before opening the shop in the mornings. He would bring him a little food and a saucer of warm milk, wait until he had finished eating and was settled, and then place a blanket over his body to keep him warm. Over the course of the day, when the shop was free of customers, he would quickly pop upstairs to check on him.

It was during one of those short absences that Beth happened to return. Finding the shop empty she supposed that Truelove had nipped out to the storeroom, or was in the yard having a smoke, so she went up to the desk and called out:

'Hello! Is anybody there?'

When no reply came, she stepped around the desk and drew back the strip blinds to look for him. What she saw completely stunned and confounded her. For there, on the wall of the store, was her father's book collection, apparently intact, and with the books virtually in the same order on the shelves as they had been in her house. It took a few moments before the penny dropped, but finally she realised exactly what had been going on, and what he had been keeping from her. The refusing of stock — the depleted bookshelves — and the evasiveness — it all started to make sense to her now.

With her mind and emotions in turmoil, she turned and rushed to leave the shop. Just as she reached the door, Truelove reappeared from upstairs, and he could tell immediately that something was wrong.

Beth was tearful, and looked tired and drawn.

'I never asked for charity!' she said reproachfully. 'You were meant to sell them.'

The bookseller instantly put two and two together. He attempted to explain, but she cut him short.

'Don't!' she said. 'I can't deal with this right now. I'll come back tomorrow and we'll sort it out then.'

And with that she was gone.

Truelove was entirely dejected. This was not the way he had planned it, or the reaction he'd imagined. He really wasn't in the frame of mind to be bothered with customers, and would gladly have closed the shop there and then; but, through force of habit, or a self-imposed sense of duty, he couldn't quite bring himself to desert his post. The rare trysts in the café were brief and guilt-ridden pleasures but, other than those, and Christmas and New Year's Day, the bookshop was always open. So he saw the working day through to its bitter end.

He spent the evening turning the matter over in his mind, and fretting about what the next day would bring.

His intentions had been good but, when all was said and done, he had deceived Beth, and he worried that she might not be able to forgive him. He planned, rehearsed and constantly revised his explanation, trying to make it sound as favourable to himself as possible. He chain-smoked cigarettes until that, combined with mental fatigue, had his head pounding to the point where he could think no more.

That night, with a heavy heart, he carried Socrates to bed with him, and placed the cat comfortably behind the crook of his knees. In the early hours of the morning he woke and felt the urge to shift position. Normally, Socrates would take the bookseller's slightest movement as a cue to adjust his own position accordingly, and the two would slowly move and settle again in perfect synchronisation. But this time Socrates did not budge. So the bookseller gave him a nudge with his leg, but still Socrates did not react. When he didn't respond to yet another prompt, Truelove sat up and pulled the bedclothes back.

'Socrates?'

He shook the cat with his hand.

'Socrates!'

But Socrates was beyond responding. He was quite cold and lifeless.

Part of the bookseller died in that moment too. In his head he knew that this day would inevitably come, and yet, paradoxically, he could never conceive of it actually happening. But it had. And now there would always be a gaping chasm in his life, a void that could never be filled. For some time he just sat in a state of dazed despondence, gently stroking his beloved pet's side. He might have remained there for quite some time had not the noise of the milk van in the street below roused him from his stupor.

He got out of bed and dressed in a perfunctory and enervated manner, then made his way downstairs and into the street. He walked through the town centre, down to the seafront, and along the promenade, until eventually he came to the stretch of beach on the very edge of the town. There he rummaged amongst the rocks until he found a small, elongated boulder to suit his purpose.

The kitchen lights were already on in the café as he passed it on his way back, and the staff busy making preparations for the day ahead. Lying on his own doorstep, beside the pint of milk, was a parcel of fresh fish for Socrates. A pang of anguish cut through him like a knife, and he hurried to open the door and step past it.

For the next couple of hours or so, he paced backwards and forwards across the living room floor, or sat on the settee, with his head bowed, smoking one cigarette after another in quick succession, and periodically checking his watch. At nine o'clock on the dot, he went out again, this time to the hardware shop a few doors up, where he bought a spade.

The Last Days of Socrates

Returning to the bookshop, he took the spade to the grassy patch at the end of the yard, and began to dig. When he considered the job done, he went back upstairs to the bedroom, and gently and lovingly lifted Socrates into an old shoe box. With great care and reverence he carried the box downstairs and out into the yard, where he buried Socrates in the little grass plot at the very back of the shop. Then he placed the boulder on top to mark the spot.

Half an hour later than normal, he opened for business.

Chapter XVI

A Proposal

ANGIE was the first through the door that morning. She browsed distractedly at the romance section for a while, occasionally glancing around at the bookseller, who was sitting at the desk with his head in his hands. When she finally picked a book, she brought it to him, and the transaction was completed in the usual laconic way. However, on this occasion, having delivered her routine 'thank you', she lingered as though she had something on her mind, something that she wanted to say. But when Truelove looked up, she just turned and left without a word.

This was to be the longest of days for the bookseller. Time dragged so slowly that it almost hurt. Every second that passed seemed like a minute, and every minute like an hour. He had to summon the will from his deepest reserves to cope with even the most basic communication with customers. If he'd had somewhere else to go, or something else to do that would help get him through the day and ease his pain, he would have been there doing it. But all he knew was the familiar routine of bookshop life; and there was, besides, the Beth situation to be resolved, so he remained at his station.

Christmas Eve made a brief appearance at the window shortly after lunchtime, announced by the rumbling of her trolley's wheels on the flagstone pavement. She stared in for a minute or so, as if to ask where the trestle tables of books were. As soon as she had moved on, Truelove went out to the front of the shop and spent some time looking in the direction from which he knew Beth would come. He noticed that the milk bottle was still on the doorstep of the flat, but that the parcel of fish had been removed.

As the day progressed he became more impatient for Beth's arrival. No matter what the outcome, he just wanted it all to be over and done with, for better or for worse.

When, at last, she did come through the door, it was late afternoon, and Truelove had no idea what to expect; but exhausted and disconsolate, he was resigned to meet his fate, whatever that might be.

But Beth was conciliatory.

'Don't look so worried!' she said. 'You know what I'm like when I'm tired and stressed, and finding those books did come as a bit of a shock. But I'm sorry that I was so petulant with you yesterday.'

Truelove acknowledged her apology with a faint, fleeting smile.

'Anyway,' she continued, 'you'd better tell me exactly

what you've been up to, although I think I have a pretty good idea already.'

The bookseller explained just as he'd rehearsed it.

'I have been paying for your mother's care in an attempt to save your father's collection,' he said. 'I know how much it means to you. But I haven't been able to return the books in the meantime in case I ultimately have no choice but to sell them.'

Beth composed herself.

'Giles Truelove,' she said, 'you are a good, good man. And I really appreciate your efforts on my behalf. But, I want you to do something for me now — and if you think anything of me at all — you will do it without question.'

Truelove waited for her to continue.

'I want you to sell those books — either by auction or through the shop — and take back whatever you are owed — or as much of it as you can get. Now, will you promise me that?'

'But, your mother's care …'

'My mother died the week before last,' Beth announced. 'On the evening of the last day we met, as it happens. That is partly why I haven't been around, and what I came to tell you yesterday. So there are no more payments to be met.'

Truelove observed how gaunt and weary she looked. The recent trauma had evidently taken its toll. He was sincerely sorry to hear the news about her mother, but didn't quite know what to say. All he could manage was the platitude 'I'm sorry for your loss.'

'It's for the best, believe me,' Beth replied. 'But sticking to the matter in hand for now — will you sell the books as I ask?'

'If that is what you really want.'

'It is. Now will you promise?'

The bookseller nodded.

Beth couldn't fail to notice how desperately despondent he seemed.

'Look Giles, if I have upset you then I am truly, deeply sorry. You are the last person on earth I'd wish to hurt. Silly woman that I am, I lash out at you as a means of coping with my stress. That's all it is — I don't really mean it.'

Truelove didn't respond.

'For goodness sake, Giles, if there's something on your mind — if you want to tell me what a cow I've been — then just spit it out!'

He paused from fiddling with the items on his desk and looked up at her.

'It's not you.'

'Well, if it's not me, then what is it?' she asked in frustration.

The bookseller simply lowered his head.

Then it suddenly struck her that there was only one other likely cause of his being in this state.

'It's not Socrates, is it?' she asked apprehensively.

Truelove pinched the top of his nose in an effort to maintain control.

She had her answer.

'Oh, no! Giles, I am so, so sorry!'

Uncharacteristically, swayed by grief, he unburdened himself, telling her of the events of the night. When he'd finished, he looked drained and broken. Beth rushed around the desk and embraced him tightly. It was the first ever physical contact between them, and it was the first time in his life that he'd experienced any such comfort from another human being. Carried away in the emotion of the moment his inhibitions simply dissolved and all his defences fell in an instant.

'Will you marry me, Beth?' he suddenly blurted out.

Beth stepped back in shock.

'I can't!' she declared, almost irascibly. 'I'm sorry — I just can't!'

Truelove's rash and unexpected proposal only succeeded in discomfiting her and in precipitating her departure.

She lingered for a moment at the door to deliver the parting words,

'Forgive me.'

Chapter XVII

The Caretaker

I had a lot of work to do before the flat would be properly habitable and the shop ready for opening. The premises were in need of such a major overhaul after so many years of neglect that I had to be there constantly in order to have any hope of finishing within the short timescale that necessity demanded. Every day that I went beyond my deadline would cost me in terms of debt, and that was something I obviously wished to avoid, if at all possible.

At lunchtimes I would go to the café next door to get some much needed sustenance, and I took the opportunity to enquire about my predecessor in the shop. The café owner and most of the staff weren't able to tell me very much other than he had kept himself to himself and that the circumstances of his death were rather tragic. It was not until Angie served me that I began to discover something more substantial about him. When I asked her what he was like she actually sat down with me for a few minutes and seemed pleased to have the chance to speak of him. Over the course of the next few weeks she would join me if she was on a break and tell me a little more of what she knew of the bookseller's life.

It was from Angie that I found out that he'd grown up in the orphanage. On first mentioning his name to her mother the woman was noticeably taken aback. She had been to school with a boy called Truelove and, from what Angie told her of the bookseller, it was established that it had to be the same person. According to Angie's mother he seemed a very lonely, isolated little boy. She was a year below him, but remembered him distinctly. While all the other children ran about and played at lunchtimes, he would sit quietly on his own reading a book. She did not recall seeing him once interact with another child. The boys and girls from the orphanage were often cruelly teased about their situation and tended to remain apart anyway, but Truelove didn't appear to communicate even with them.

I asked Angie if she knew of anyone who had worked at the orphanage during those years and might be able to cast some light on how he came to be there and what happened to him after he left, because there were many years unaccounted for before he eventually opened the shop. But she didn't. The institution had closed long ago and had been demolished to make way for a supermarket. She suggested that the older residents of the town were more likely to provide a lead and that she would start by asking her mother that evening.

The Caretaker

Angie's mum was only a girl herself at that time and had no reason to know who had worked at the orphanage, but in due course she mentioned it to her own mother who subsequently asked among *her* friends and contemporaries. That eventually produced the desired result. I was given the name of the long-serving caretaker of the children's home and was pointed in the general direction of where he lived. I took an afternoon break from my renovations and went to the housing estate where I was told he could be found. Not having an exact address for him meant that I had to wander about making enquiries of passers-by and in the local shops, but, finally, I managed to pin down his location to a particular street. There, I went from door to door, until a young woman kindly volunteered to lead me right to his house.

I knocked at the door, waited, but got no answer. I knocked again, but still no one came. After getting no response to a third and fourth attempt I assumed that he was out and was in the process of walking back down the path when I heard the door open behind me.

'Mr Southwick?' I asked of the elderly gentleman who was standing there in his vest and braces.

'Yes.'

'I'm told that you were once the caretaker at the local orphanage?'

'Maybe,' he replied cautiously. 'Who's asking?'

I told him my name and that I had just taken over a shop in town.

'I'm hoping that you might be able to help me,' I said. 'I'm trying to find out about the man who previously owned my shop. I believe he was at the orphanage in the 1940s and 50s — a boy called Giles Truelove.'

I caught a look of immediate recognition in his face, but the old man was wary. However, once I fully explained the situation and my motivation for asking, he seemed satisfied and put at his ease.

'You'd better come in,' he said.

He took me into his front parlour and offered me a cup of tea, which I accepted out of politeness. I looked about me while he was in the kitchen. On the sideboard was an array of old black and white family photographs, with pride of place in the centre given to a kindly looking lady who I assumed had been his wife and had since passed on. The subtle touches of a female's presence in a house, not always obvious or easy to define, were entirely absent here. The ticking of an old wooden-cased Napoleon mantel clock seemed inordinately loud and languorous in the otherwise still and silent room, and it gave the illusion of time moving more slowly here than in the outside world.

Mr Southwick returned carrying a tray laden with teapot, china cups and saucers, milk jug, sugar bowl, teaspoons, and a small plate displaying an array of biscuits that only the older generation would still buy. I imagined that this was a little ceremony that his wife had performed when visitors came and that he was simply continuing the ritual. Consciously or subconsciously, it was a small act of remembrance on his part.

When we were settled I asked if he knew how Truelove came to be in the orphanage in the first place, and that's when he told me about the bookseller's parents being killed in the Blitz. He clearly recalled him arriving at the home as he was in the process of cleaning the light covers and replacing broken bulbs in the entrance hall that afternoon. He saw the boy step through the door with a battered little suitcase for luggage.

'The poor wee mite looked so lost and forlorn,' he said. 'Later on I remarked on this to a member of staff and she was the one who told me his story, or what she knew of it. After he lost his parents, and no relatives were found to take him in, he was adopted by a couple somewhere out in the country; but the husband was in the army and got killed in the very last days of the war. What I heard was that his wife went to pieces after that and couldn't cope with the farm, or the boy. She had some sort of breakdown, you see, so he was put back into care, and that's how he ended up with us.'

'When he was older,' he continued, 'he used to run errands for me and I'd give him a few pennies for his trouble.

He was always arriving back with books — he had books on the brain, that boy! Books, books, books! I kept them in an unused storeroom for him as the children were only allowed a small bedside locker in the dormitories. Then when the time came for him to leave the home he came to me and asked if I'd continue to look after his books until he could get back to collect them, and I agreed. I never thought that it would take nearly fifteen years! What's more, in the meantime I started to receive parcels every so often with a note inside saying "Please keep safe — GJT". More books!!'

The old man smiled and shook his head.

'Anyway, one lunchtime I was sitting in the caretaker's room munching away on my sandwiches when a man appears at the door and just stands there looking at me. Doesn't say a word — just stands there. "Yes?" says I. "Can I help you?" "I've come to collect my books," he says, and for a moment I'm looking at him wondering what the blue blazes he's talking about. Then, as he stands there staring at me, and I'm gaping back blankly at him, the penny suddenly drops and I realize who it must be. Stupidly, in my head I'd always expected the boy to come back for his books, not a man. I didn't recognize him. It took a while for me to get my head round it. I asked him how he was and he just said "Well", then I led him to the storeroom where his books were kept and opened it for him. He had a van parked outside, filled with empty boxes, and I offered to help him pack the books and load it, but he refused. So I just stood and watched as he went back and forth until the job was done. Nobody else was about, as they were all off at the canteen at that time of day, and I guess that's the way he planned it. As he was about to leave, the two of us stood beside the van gazing at each other in awkward silence for what seemed like an age. Then he gives me a nod, gets into the vehicle, drives off, and that's the last I ever see of him. That man didn't say "Goodbye" or utter so much as a "Thank you", but he didn't need to. I could see the gratitude in his eyes and I could read it in his heart. The poor soul just didn't know how to express it.'

'Did he tell you where he was — what he'd been doing — all those years?' I asked.

'Ah, no, he didn't — but I knew nevertheless.'

'Oh?'

'He was in the army.'

'The army?' I repeated with surprise.

'Yes. It wasn't hard to figure out. I noticed that he was wearing service shoes for a start, and the clothes he had on him looked for all the world like a demob suit. Everything about him just smacked of the military. It was a bit like the children at the home — you would know where they came from without having to be told — their clothes, their haircuts, and even they way they spoke, were all giveaway signs.'

'Are you sure about that?' I asked, '… and it was definitely the army?'

Mr Southwick chuckled.

'Yes, I'm perfectly sure. I could tell straightaway, but seeing his kitbag in the back of the van only confirmed it. It was labelled with his name and regiment.'

I left Mr Southwick, having thanked him for his help and hospitality, and made my way back to the shop on a bus.

It came as a shock to learn that Truelove had served so long in the army. Knowing what I did of the man, it hardly seemed credible that he would choose a regimented military life. I thought his intellectual leanings would have legislated against it. But, after turning it over in my mind for a while, it occurred to me that it was really a perfectly logical choice in the circumstances. He would have received no more than a good, but rudimentary formal education, so his options would have been limited in the first place. Then, having spent his childhood in an orphanage, the transition to a barrack block environment would not have proved particularly traumatic for him. It was simply a question of swapping one institutional life for another.

With free food, clothes and accommodation, and no

utility bills to pay, the army also afforded him the opportunity to save money to a degree not possible in civilian life. It all began to fall into place now. He'd been working to a plan all along, and had been prepared to sacrifice his youth and freedom in order to pursue a dream.

When the time came, he returned to the only place he really knew, and there, shortly afterwards, he invested in a quaint little double-fronted shop in a side-street close to the town centre. It was a building that he remembered fondly and it was opportune that it happened to be for sale at the time.

Chapter XVIII

Forgiveness

TRUELOVE was in no mood to forgive Beth. She had flounced out on him once too often. He'd suffered enough anguish from the relationship to last him a lifetime. Moreover, he was convinced that he'd been taken for a complete fool and that she had merely used him when there was nothing better on offer. She was never going to marry him, and he was deluded for ever thinking that she would. By now she probably had a professional man in her sights — a doctor, dentist or accountant — a widower she'd met at church — so his friendship had been conveniently dispensed with. In fact, he'd played right into her hands and made it perfectly easy for her. How callous she had been to lead him on then reject him when at his most vulnerable. The loss of Socrates was devastating enough, but she had managed to compound his sorrow many times over.

As in the past, faced with an emotional crisis, he immersed himself in work as a coping mechanism, and resolved never to be drawn into anything more than the most basic communication with another human being ever again. The first thing he did was to start processing her father's books and put them out for sale in the shop. He priced them in anger and took no pleasure in the task.

He trawled through volumes of the *Book Auction Records* and specialist catalogues to find values for the scarcer items, and where no record could be found he made an educated guess, or held the book aside for future research. Most of the books were, of course, old familiars to him, and he was able to price those quickly. There were *Baedekkers*; volumes from the *Highways and Byways* series; most of the *King's England* books, edited by Arthur Mee; a run of Batsford's *The Face of Britain* publications, and almost a complete set of 'King Penguins'.

Tins of Edgar Backus' 'Bookcloth Cleaner' and 'Leather Binding Polish' were brought down from upstairs, and Truelove sat for hours applying it gently with cotton wool to those bindings in need of a little attention. Stale bread was rubbed up and down the edges of books to remove years of engrained dust and to brighten them up a bit; and dustwrappers were slipped into lengths of Mylar jacket protection that had been carefully measured and cut from a roll.

All this occupied the bookseller for more than a week and to some degree took his mind off other matters. But it was impossible to stay distracted all the time. There were too many reminders of Socrates to be avoided — the plucked arms of the settee, scratch marks on the doors, his favourite sleeping spots — they were constant and everywhere, and triggered waves of sadness. In moments of forgetfulness Truelove would leave doors ajar to allow the cat to go in and out at his leisure, and he continued to move cautiously in bed at nights so as not to disturb him.

As for Beth, he found himself thinking of her involuntarily, try as he might to eradicate her completely from his mind. It annoyed and frustrated him that he was unable to control his own thoughts and that through this weakness she could even yet maintain a foothold in his life. All his memories of her, even those moments that were pleasurable at the time, now assumed a negative interpretation.

For a good number of months he survived off his anger. It kept him going and got him through the days. But that intensity of anger is impossible to sustain permanently, especially when it is merely the manifestation of other emotions disguised, and gradually, through time, it inevitably begins to abate. And so it did in the bookseller's case. He started to consider matters from an entirely different perspective, and he began to question his own behaviour and doubt his earlier conclusions. He had asked Beth to marry him when she had just lost her mother, when she was distressed and grieving. His timing could not have been worse or more insensitive. And even if his suspicions about there being someone else were well-founded, it was her life at the end of the day, and her choice. You cannot force somebody to reciprocate feelings. So, really, what right had he to be angry at her refusal?

The truth is that Truelove understood loneliness for the first time in his life. Socrates was gone, and he missed Beth's company. He could not bring Socrates back, but there was still a chance that he could salvage his friendship with Beth. He decided that it would be better to see her occasionally, as a friend, than never at all, and so he resolved to make contact with her again. Perhaps the situation was beyond repair, and he would get rebuffed, but he would try nonetheless. At the very least he wanted the opportunity to say his piece, and get 'closure' as the Americans would say.

So, on the evening of his resolution, he walked to her house with the intention of clearing the air. The house was entirely in darkness and there were no signs of life, but he knocked anyway. He was extremely tense, nervous, and fearful of her reaction, so when no answer came he felt strangely relieved. Nevertheless, despite his misgivings, once he'd determined on this course of action he felt an overwhelming compulsion to see it through, almost as though his mind had been possessed and his free will subjugated.

He tried again on the following evening, but with the same result. On Sunday he stationed himself along from her church, and out of sight, thinking that he might catch her on her way home; but there was no sign of her among the dispersing congregation. When the last stragglers and all hope had gone he made his way wearily back to the shop.

He called at the house for a third time during the course of the next week, but again she was not at home. By this stage he knew that there was something amiss because she had not been in the habit of going out at night, or of missing church. In all likelihood she was on a holiday, or visiting a friend or relative, although he couldn't help but speculate for the worse. Perhaps she had indeed found a man with whom she was spending her evenings and weekends, or had even moved in with him already. But, whatever her position, he still wanted the opportunity to speak to her, if only for a last time. He thought about knocking at Dorothy's door, but his courage failed him. So, once again, he returned to the shop frustrated.

On enquiring the next day at her place of work he was told that she had quit her job some time ago, which only served to deepen his suspicion that someone else was supporting her. The house would be hers now, but she still needed to live somehow.

He finally decided that rather than subject himself further to the dread and disappointment in seeking her out that he would simply write a note and put it through her door.

Forgiveness

His message was short and to the point:

'Please come to see me — Giles.'

For a last time he walked to her house and, on seeing no signs of life, he posted the note through her letterbox. He had done all he could do and now the outcome was in her hands. It was a question of waiting and hoping on his part.

However, weeks passed and Beth did not come. He felt hurt beyond words that she had not responded in any way. Had he been of so little significance in her life that he wasn't even worth acknowledging? Even a 'Dear John' letter would have been better than no reply at all, for at least it would imply that his existence meant something to her. But there was nothing.

Then, one evening, as a last customer was leaving, he was about to shut the shop door and turn the sign on it to 'closed' when a genial looking lady in her late fifties or early sixties approached as though to make her way in.

'I'm just closing,' said the bookseller. 'Is there something in particular that you wanted?'

'There is,' the woman replied. 'I take it that you are Giles — Giles Truelove?'

Truelove was rather disconcerted at her knowing his name. She had him at a disadvantage.

'Yes?'

'I'm Dorothy,' she said, 'Beth's next door neighbour.'

He was completely taken aback by the announcement

and apprehensive about what it might signify. He stood gaping at her for a few seconds before collecting himself and stepping aside to let her pass.

'There's no easy way of saying this,' she began once inside, then hesitated momentarily before declaring:

'Beth's gone.'

She looked searchingly at Truelove to see if he had fully grasped her meaning, but he seemed uncertain.

'She passed away Tuesday week ago,' Dorothy continued, 'peacefully in her sleep.'

The bookseller showed no visible reaction at all, but a thunderbolt could not have hit him harder.

'I'm so very sorry,' she added in the most compassionate of tones.

The trauma of the news rendered Truelove temporarily stupefied and inert while his mind struggled to cope with the enormity of it. When he did eventually manage to speak it was to utter one word — and that was breathed, and barely audible.

'How?'

'It was pancreatic cancer. She didn't want you to know. She knew how devastated you would be and wanted to spare you that. But she was in good hands, believe me. The staff at the hospice couldn't have been kinder.'

Truelove slowly made his way over to the desk and sat down behind it.

Forgiveness

'You should know that she thought the world of you,' Dorothy went on. 'She loved you more than anything. The day you proposed it really hit her hard. She had only just learned that there wasn't long to go and it broke her heart that she couldn't accept. In her eyes it was better to let you think that she'd rejected you than put you through the torment of watching her condition worsen. And you know what women are like about looking their best — especially our beautiful Beth — she couldn't bear the thought of you seeing her at the end. She wanted you to remember her as she was. She also wanted to spare you the agony of the funeral and asked me to come to see you only when it was over. So here I am.'

'But look,' she said, pulling an envelope from her pocket and handing it to him, 'she explains it all in this. And she has a special favour to ask — one last request to make of you.'

'I know it is of little consolation to you right now,' she said in conclusion, 'But things will get a little easier, given time.'

Dorothy saw herself out and left the bookseller to read the letter and begin the process of grieving.

Chapter XIX

The Letter

THE next morning Angie was busy cleaning tables when she happened to glance through the café window to see Christmas Eve standing sentinel opposite the bookshop with her trolley parked at her side. An hour or so later, when she looked again, Christmas Eve was still there, in exactly the same position, staring in the direction of the bookshop. She asked the café owner if she could take a minute and stepped outside to investigate.

It was past 11.30am and the bookshop had yet to open. In all the time that Angie had worked next door she had never known it to be closed at that hour of the day. The milk had not been lifted from the doorstep and there was no sign of activity inside the shop. Angie, like Christmas Eve, sensed that something was wrong. She knocked several times at the door to the flat, but got no response. Then she went back into the café and re-emerged with the owner. As the two of them consulted on the pavement the plumber from the premises on the other side of the bookshop appeared at his door and asked if anything was the matter. While Angie expressed her concern to him the café owner returned to her customers.

The Letter

The plumber hammered hard at the door with his fist, but that too failed to elicit a response. He and Angie were discussing what they might do next when he casually tried the handle and discovered that the door had been left unlocked. He leaned in and shouted up the stairs, but got no reply. Then he made his way into the hallway and slowly began to climb the book-lined stairs, calling out as he went, and with Angie following close behind. The door of the living room was ajar and he craned his head round it to see Truelove lying on his side on the green settee. He stepped into the room and called again as he approached the bookseller. Kneeling in front of the him, he closely examined his face before taking hold of a wrist and checking for a pulse. Then he turned to Angie, who was stationed at the door, and slowly shook his head.

Angie gasped and buried her face in her hands. It was what she had feared, but prayed wouldn't be true. The plumber got up and placed his hand on her shoulder.

'I'll go and ring for an ambulance,' he said.

The waitress was badly shaken. As she stood alone with her thoughts, surveying the scene and trying to come to terms with it, she glimpsed a letter lying on the floor behind the far corner of the settee. Collecting herself, she went to retrieve it, moving forward cautiously and quietly, as though afraid to disturb the bookseller from his sleep. Gently pulling the letter from its envelope, she began to read, and as she read her eyes began to well with tears. Then, on hearing footsteps on the stairs, she quickly slipped the letter back into its envelope, and tucked it into her apron pocket.

Chapter XX

The Grand Opening

THE day of my grand opening finally came. I had put an enormous amount of effort into preparing my little shop for this moment and had already grown extremely attached to it. I stepped outside and stood proudly before it with the keys in my hand, looking up at the refurbished wooden sign. It was painted in gold lettering on a black background, and read: 'G. J. Truelove, Bookseller — Est. 1969 — Books bought & sold'.

What better tribute could I pay the man for whom I had so much admiration and respect and who had given me a sense of direction when I had none? It was as though fate had decreed that I should find his journal and be inspired to carry the bookshop tradition into a third generation. He had introduced me to a world of which I had previously known nothing, and I quickly came to understand the magic and beauty of it all. The connection with it is not something that can be learned, but felt in the heart or soul only. It cannot be described or explained to those who do not feel it — it is either there or it is not there; and, fortunately, for me it was there.

I advertised in the window for stock, and in the local newspapers. The response was good. Many of Truelove's former customers made their way to me and sold what they had bought from him and no longer wanted to keep, and it was strange to think that what had once passed through his hands would now pass through mine. I also made a point of acquiring some of the bookseller's favourite tools of the trade — McKerrow's *An Introduction to Bibliography for Literary Students*, Slater's *How to Collect Books*, Carter's *ABC for Book Collectors*. And, of course, how could I not secure a copy of his most loved book, and now one of mine — *The Private Papers of a Bankrupt Bookseller*.

Truelove's tale was in many ways a sad one, but there was consolation in it too. For although he died broken-hearted, he died in the knowledge that he had been loved. He had loved in turn, both Socrates and Beth, and by loving he had lived.

On a bookcase, in the living room above the shop, Truelove's journal and Beth's diary sit side by side, together forever, or for my lifetime at least. I had visited Dorothy to hear her account of the story and, in the course of conversation, she produced the diary that she had rescued from Beth's house. She could think of no more fitting place for it than to rest beside the bookseller's journal.

I owed so much to Angie too. For she could not have been more helpful in my quest to piece together the bookseller's story. She had grown fond of Truelove over time, and wanted to please him if she could, but feared that any overt show of kindness might be construed as pity, and would not have been well received. I do not doubt that she was right. Leaving the parcels of fish for Socrates was her way of doing something for him without causing offence.

On the morning that Socrates died she had watched Truelove bury him from the upstairs window at the back of the café. When the moment was right, she slipped out and removed the fish that she had left that morning, knowing how he would feel to see it there. Her heart went out to him, but she had no idea what to do or say for the best.

However, she knew that he had Beth for comfort, and it had pleased her no end to see them together in the café, enjoying each other's company. She was gratified to see the bookseller happy, for she rightly sensed that behind that gruff exterior lay a kind and delicate soul. It was in relating the events surrounding his death that she first mentioned his name to her mother and discovered that he had spent his childhood in the orphanage. She broke down and cried uncontrollably in sorrow and pity for the man.

When I appeared in the café and asked about him, she was only too pleased to tell me what she knew. It was an unburdening, an act of catharsis for her. Talking to someone else who cared about the bookseller's story gave her a means to purge her sorrow. I must confess that I nearly cried myself when she showed me Beth's letter, which had the poem 'Remember' by Christina Rossetti appended at the end. Angie still had no idea why she had taken it as she did, but I was glad that she had, for she saw to it that Beth's last wish was fulfilled.

I promised Angie that she would be my first paying customer when I opened the shop for business. So, come 9 o'clock on that morning, I arranged to meet her outside and held the door open to let her enter. I went and sat behind the desk and left her to browse contentedly at the romance section. When she had picked what she wanted she came over and handed the book to me. I checked the price inside and said 'One ninety-five!' She smiled, took her purse from her apron pocket, and gave me the exact change. As I looked up at her I was struck by the beautiful softness about those beguiling brown eyes of hers.

Remember

Remember me when I am gone away,
Gone far away into the silent land;
When you can no more hold me by the hand,
Nor I half turn to go yet turning stay.
Remember me when no more day by day
You tell me of our future that you plann'd:
Only remember me; you understand
It will be late to counsel then or pray.
Yet if you should forget me for a while
And afterwards remember, do not grieve:
For if the darkness and corruption leave
A vestige of the thoughts that once I had,
Better by far you should forget and smile
Than that you should remember and be sad.

Christina Rossetti

Epilogue

All Souls

On a bright Sunday afternoon in September, at the end of my first week in business, Angie and I walked to All Souls Church and stopped before a grave in the burial-ground. The inscription on the headstone read:

> Elizabeth Jane Grayson
> 1944-1987
> Beloved daughter of Gladys and Rendell
> In God's care

We paused before it for a while, then Angie gave my hand a gentle squeeze before walking a little further along the path to allow me a few moments to myself. I looked across to the adjacent grave. Lying horizontally on it, in a perspex plaque, was an old Victorian bookmark with a golden tassel. And on the headstone that I had commissioned were the words:

> Giles James Truelove
> Bookseller
> 1939-1987
> Dearest friend of Elizabeth Grayson
> Gone, but not forgotten

'You got your wish, Beth,' I said. 'You got your wish.'

When Angie returned to my side, she slipped her arm around my waist and rested her head on my shoulder, then we turned and made our way slowly towards the cemetery gates.

Printed in Great Britain
by Amazon

28214175R00076